the ANGRY ATHEIST

the ANGRY ATHEIST

JOHNNY GIESBRECHT

MOODY PRESS
CHICAGO

© 1976 by
THE MOODY BIBLE INSTITUTE
OF CHICAGO

Library of Congress Cataloging in Publication Data

Giesbrecht, Johnny.
  The angry atheist.

  SUMMARY: A profoundly Christian teen-ager encounters a
skeptical atheistic neighbor.
  [1. Christian life—Fiction] I. Title.
PZ7.C3624An [Fic] 75-38709

ISBN 0-8024-0223-2

Printed in the United States of America

Contents

1

A Splinter of Glass

It was quitting time for Don Shield, or it would have been if the maniac hadn't broken loose from Ward Four. As it was, Don soon found himself busier than he had been all day.

Eighteen-year-old Don had been doing volunteer work at the Minneapolis Mental Institution for several months. The Saturday afternoons he spent there were full of action, teaching swimming and water safety to some of the male patients. Don's swimming skills were excellent; he had just completed his senior year in high school and already had a lifeguard certificate. But he sometimes had to wonder about other qualifications.

Although he didn't need a degree in psychiatry, Don knew that this project was no ordinary swimming class. Its main purpose was to gain the confidence of a dozen mixed-up adults who had blown their minds on all sorts of problems. Some of the men had attempted suicide, and one in the group had

killed his own brother in a fit of insane rage. The more
one learned about the men—as Don did from the
orderlies and from the patients themselves—the more
it made one's hair bristle. But Don knew that the men
in his class had made progress toward restoration.
The worst patients never got close to the pool; they
were kept in Ward Four under especially strict super-
vision.

Don had already changed from trunks and gym
shirt to faded blue jeans and matching waist-length
denim jacket. The jacket was short enough so that it
didn't cover his wide belt which was made of shiny
black leather and sported an oval, nickel-plated har-
ness buckle. He wore black cavalry boots, complete
with rings and straps.

Don was tall, and the close-fitting jeans and short
jacket emphasized his slender, broad-shouldered,
athletic build. He walked straight and held his chest
high. All of his movements had a smooth, clean-cut,
decisive quality about them, so that he gave a con-
stant impression of immense self-confidence. This
aura of strength never seemed to leave him, even
when he was tired or in a bad mood.

He was tired now as he walked down the gloomy,
dark-paneled corridor toward the stairwell that
would take him down five floors to street level. He
hoped he wouldn't have to wait too long for a bus.

Don came to a sharp stop near the stairway door
when he heard angry shouting in the hallway behind
him. He turned and saw a man come running toward

him, but still a good distance away. Don knew it was
one of the patients from Ward Four, not only because
of the special gray uniform which all the most difficult inmates wore, but because of the way he was
waving his arms about madly as he ran. And the
man's face, so distorted by insane rage, was horrible
to see.

Don's scalp prickled, but his chest came up higher
and his shoulders squared. As a regular member of
the volunteer program, he felt duty bound to do his
best to stop this runaway patient from hurting himself
or others; but actually Don's thoughts about what he
should do wouldn't have been any different if he had
been a visitor in the place. It was Don's way to stand
up straight in the face of any challenge; however, at
present he wasn't overly confident that he could
handle the situation. The approaching maniac was
tall and wiry-looking, and the manic state he was in
would multiply his natural strength.

So Don was relieved when a couple of white-coated
orderlies rounded the corner at the far end of the
corridor and came running in pursuit. Still shouting
curses, the fleeing mental patient looked back over
his shoulder and increased his speed. But when he
was only a few yards away from Don, he came to a
sliding stop and quickly ducked into another hallway. It led to a ward where the most recovered and
easily managed patients were kept.

Don ran forward now and met the two orderlies at
the hallway intersection as they swung around the

corner in hot pursuit. Don fell into step beside them, and one of them told him, "Markham got away from us while we were taking him back from the showers. He's in a very violent state, so we'll need all the help we can get in grabbing him and holding him down."

The runaway didn't have much farther to go before he came to the end of the hallway and a heavy oaken door that barred the entrance to Ward Seven. This door, like almost all in the building, was kept locked. But then, just as the raving man got there, it swung open and showed a lone orderly standing there with his key in his hand. Maybe he had heard the shouting and had come through to see what was happening. In a flash the patient had charged past the orderly, causing him to stagger back off balance. The patient dashed on into the large room which was the center of Ward Seven.

Perhaps a dozen small round tables were scattered about the room, and they had already been set for an early supper. As Don and the orderlies raced through the doorway they saw the fleeing man cutting across the room in a zigzag line and taking time to upset every table that wasn't too far out of reach from the roughly diagonal course he was following. In his wake the tile floor was a mess of food and broken dishes.

From a far corner of the large room an open doorway led into a long, narrow chamber that was brightly illuminated with sunlight shining in through a row of large windows which were made up of many small panes in wooden frames. They were the only windows in the whole building that were not barred with steel. The patients in Ward Seven weren't violent, so they didn't really need any barred windows; and the sun-room, where they could sit at the long table and work at various crafts, was definitely the most cheerful spot in the whole hospital.

The runaway patient from Ward Four headed for this room. He ducked in through the door and disappeared from the sight of his pursuers, but Don and the orderlies hurried across the large room, sidestepping tables and chairs, and trying not to slip in lemon pudding. There were about thirty mental patients lounging about the room; they all stood or sat very still as they watched this sudden excitement.

Don and the two orderlies crowded through the doorway into the sun-room just in time to see Markham near the far end of the room, swinging a chair at the window. Glass shattered and wood splintered, and Markham had a hole big enough to crawl through. He hopped up on the windowsill and got one leg through the hole. Then he yelled at his pursuers who had now almost reached him, "Stop! Stop or I'll jump!"

Don and the others came to a halt about twenty feet away from the man. All three were convinced that the distraught inmate would have flung himself out into space immediately if they hadn't obeyed. Suicide attempts weren't altogether uncommon among the patients from Ward Four. Through the broken window

came the sound of heavy after-work traffic five floors
down.

The poor maniac, squatting there on the windowsill with one foot through the jagged hole in the glass,
was a frightful sight to see. Twisted ropes of black
hair hung over a hollow-cheeked face that was distorted terribly by confused emotions of fear, rage, and
hatred. He held his long, thin arms out slightly
akimbo, for he was in a state of extreme tenseness,
ready to fling himself backward to a horrible death
fifty feet below.

One of the orderlies began to speak in a calm voice.
"We're your friends, Bradley. You don't have to be
afraid of us. Why were you running away?"

"Friends!" snorted Bradley Markham. "You're not
my friends!"

"Of course we are," insisted the orderly.

"Then why are you always trying to kill me?" asked
Markham. Don noticed for the first time that the
patient's hands were trembling.

"Bradley," said the orderly, "we have not been
trying to kill you. We've been trying to help you in
every way we can, and we're going to—"

"You don't want to just kill me—you're not satisfied with that!" accused the patient. "You want to
torture me to death slowly! Don't try to fool me! I
know that's what you've been trying to do ever since I
came here."

"Bradley, we're your friends. Now come down off
that windowsill. It's time to go to supper."

But Bradley's face grew more distorted with the awful conflict going on inside him. "I know you want to torture me to death! Today you were going to drown me under the showers!" He carried on like that for about half a minute, relating the various types of death and torture he imagined the orderlies had already attempted to inflict on him, and also throwing in a few that he supposed they would try before long.

Don was getting a bit bored with the whole thing. It seemed to him that the orderlies were fooling around. One quick dash, thought Don, and they could get to the man and pull him down off the sill before he had a chance to jump through the window. While the patient was still garbling away, Don spoke in a low voice to the orderly standing next to him. "Let's grab him."

The orderly was a big, well-built man, and he didn't seem to be the kind of person who would be afraid of action, but his almost-whispered answer to Don was: "No way! He means what he says. He'd fling himself out through that window before we got halfway over to him. Just leave him to me. But stay here in case we need your help once we get him to come down out of the window."

Don glanced backward over his shoulder and saw that several orderlies were standing in the doorway watching, but they didn't dare step any closer for fear of further upsetting the patient.

The orderly who stood next to Don continued his effort to calm Markham, but Markham became more and more abusive in his condemning of the treatment

he claimed to have been receiving at the hands of the
orderlies, until his tirade deteriorated into outright
cursing—a long string of it. He called the orderlies
just about everything that a person does not like to be
called. Then he went back to relating more instances
of attempted murder and torture on the part of the
hospital staff.

Both orderlies standing beside Don continued to
look relaxed and patient, but Don was growing more
restless with every passing second. *What a waste of
time!* he thought. *I could easily dash over to that
nitwit and grab him before he knew what was coming
off. He'd never get a chance to jump. And here we are,
standing around!*

Don held himself back for another two minutes or
so, then he made up his mind to put an end to this
nonsense, no matter what the orderly said. He'd probably be pretty mad at first, but when he saw that Don
had brought everything under control he'd have to
thank him.

So Don edged away to the side, putting distance
between the big orderly and himself. But as Don lowered his shoulders slightly in preparation to make the
sudden dash, the orderly reached out with the speed
of an attacking snake and grabbed him by the arm.
The grip was like a tight circle of steel.

"All right, Don," said the orderly, "you're not helping here at all, so out you go." He yanked the youth
backward a step before releasing him. "You heard
me—get out of here!"

For a few seconds Don stood still, deciding whether or not to obey, then he turned and walked toward the doorway. The group standing there made room for him to pass through, but he came to a stop in their midst and turned about to see how things would come out.

Markham began to laugh loudly. "They've got your number now!" he said. After a moment Don realized that the patient was talking to him. "You'd better run for your life while you can! They'll try to drown you under the showers! And they'll put poison in your food to make you sick! That's what they did to me! And I'd sooner die than go through that torture again!" He turned his head and looked down at the street below and then moved a little farther into the jagged hole.

What a chance! thought Don. *While he's looking the other way they could easily rush him.* But he knew they wouldn't.

The big orderly said, "Bradley, your mother will be coming to visit you again tomorrow. She's always so happy to see you."

Bradley turned his face back to the room and stared straight ahead. His face relaxed into a blank expression for a moment, but then it twisted up again as he began to cry. Squatting there on the windowsill with his long arms hanging down lower than his feet, Bradley Markham cried as vociferously as any little baby and his cheeks grew wet with tears. Now the two orderlies began to walk slowly toward him.

Markham continued to cry as they reached him, but when the big orderly put an arm around his shoulders he calmed down to the point of sniffling, with only a sob now and then.

"Everything's going to be all right, Bradley," encouraged the orderly. "Your mom wants you to eat regularly. You know she told you that, so let's go and have a good supper now. I think there's lemon pudding tonight—your favorite."

"Is there lemon pudding?" sniffled Bradley.

"Yes, there is." They helped him down off the windowsill and led him toward the doorway. Everyone there, including Don, cleared the way by hurrying into the big room.

Don made a fast circle around the upset tables and headed for the exit. He was embarrassed at the way the orderly had spoken to him, actually telling him to get out of the room! Everyone standing there had heard it. And now that the orderly had managed to calm the patient, he looked entirely justified in what he had said.

They were just lucky! Don told himself. He groped in his pocket for the key that had been issued to him when he became a regular volunteer worker. Don unlocked the oaken door, stepped through, and let it snap shut behind him without looking back. He knew the orderlies bringing the patient would be there in a few seconds and would have to unlock the door again, but that was their problem. He just wanted to get out of here. And maybe he wouldn't come back either.

Three minutes of striding through corridors, descending stairways, and passing through several more locked doors, brought Don out into a pleasantly cool evening, exceptionally cool for late June. There was a smell of moisture in the air, and the sky was partly overcast, but so far no rain was falling and the descending sun was still thrusting its golden rays between the high buildings of downtown Minneapolis.

Don's bus stop was only half a block from the mental institution. Several people were standing there waiting when Don arrived. Something was going on; everyone's eyes were focused on two of the people, a young man in a fancy red and white western shirt and a dark-haired girl who could have been fifteen or sixteen years old. The girl, wearing a blue skirt and short-sleeved white blouse, was holding her arm just above the wrist as though she was hurt. The young man stood very close to her, apparently in sympathy, and soon Don was near enough to be able to hear his words.

"Has the bleeding stopped?"

"Yes," replied the girl. "Stop worrying, it's only a scratch."

Don wondered if the girl's wound might have been caused by the glass falling from the window that Markham had smashed on the fifth floor. This was unlikely though, for there was a wide lawn area be-

tween the sidewalk and the institution building. Still,
Don felt obligated to find out for sure. He walked up to
the couple.

"Hi," he said, looking down at the girl's dark-
tanned, delicately featured face. "What happened to
your arm?"

She smiled up at him with a look of completely
innocent friendliness, like a little girl of five might if
her mother hadn't yet told her about the dangers of
speaking to strangers. Her eyes, slightly widened
with surprise, were dark and beautiful. A tiny round
birthmark was on her left cheek. She was short,
small-boned, and slim-waisted, and the fact that she
was hurt made Don want to put his arms around her to
comfort her. She said, "I'm not sure what happened,
except that some glass came falling down from
somewhere. But it's not serious. See?" She held her
arm up to Don and he decided that she was right; it
wasn't a bad cut.

He told her, "You'd better get somewhere where
you can have it disinfected and a bandage put on it."

The youth in the cowboy shirt said, "I guess a
window broke in that building back there." He
pointed. "We were taking a shortcut across the lawn
because we didn't want to miss the next bus, and the
first thing we knew, splinters of glass were raining
down on us." He appeared to be about Don's age but
had wider shoulders; in fact, he was exceptionally
large-framed and muscular. His sandy hair was a little

shorter than the way most boys his age wore it. His straight-featured face was remarkably handsome.

Don wondered if this couple was going steady; then his sharp eye noted that in spite of the difference in coloring, there was a definite resemblance between them. *They could be brother and sister,* thought Don, *or maybe cousins.*

Don said, "I was in the room where the window broke."

"Oh?" The youth looked quite surprised. "What happened?"

"That building is a mental hospital," said Don. "One of the patients was thinking of killing himself, so he smashed the window with a chair. He was going to jump out."

The girl gasped, as did some of the older ladies in the group standing around waiting for the bus and listening to the conversation. Don continued, "We stopped him before he could jump. I work there." He felt that he had been fairly honest in saying "we stopped him." For, after all, as a member of the volunteer program he worked with the regular staff, and it was staff members who had brought Markham under control.

The other youth looked at the girl. "I guess we were pretty lucky, Julie," he said. "We just had a little glass falling on us, but it could have been a man."

"Right," said Julie. "Y'know, it's kind of strange when you stop to think of it. One of the reasons we were so anxious to go on this trip was so we could get away from a mentally ill person, at least temporarily, and now we came close to having one drop on our heads!"

"Yeah," said her partner.

Don found these two very interesting, especially the girl. "My name is Don Shield," he said. "Don't you live around here then?"

The young man laughed a little. "No," he said, "not exactly. We're from Saskatchewan, Canada. My name is Pete Simmons, and this is my sister, Julie."

It was silly, but Don had to restrain himself from letting out a sigh of relief. "Glad to meet you," he said, "and welcome to Minnesota. Now listen, you ought to go back to the institution and tell them what happened. I think they'd be willing to compensate you for what happened; they certainly should."

"No," said Julie, "I wouldn't trouble them for such a little thing. I'm just glad that man didn't jump out."

Pete said, "I find it interesting that you work in a mental hospital. You probably know quite a bit about mentally ill people."

"Not really," admitted Don. "Actually I work there only on Saturday afternoons, as a volunteer."

"That's great," said Pete, and his open face showed he was being sincere.

Don had never been one to hold back from expressing his spiritual beliefs to others, not even to complete strangers. "I work there because I feel that's what the Lord wants me to do. I'm a follower of Jesus."

Pete's face, which had been cheerful enough before, now lit up like a lamp being turned to full power. "Well, I sure am glad to hear that! That's great! Julie and I are Christians too!"

For a few seconds the three just stood there in silent surprise, wondering what this strange meeting —brought about by a falling splinter of glass—might lead to.

Just then Don's bus pulled up. It happened to be the same one that the two Canadians had been waiting for. As they moved into line to board the bus, Don asked them how long they planned to stay in Minneapolis.

"About a week," said Pete. "We're visiting relatives. But we may spend some of that time at a lake. I hear your state has 10,000 to choose from."

"They used to say we had 10,000," said Don, "but lately they've rounded up about 5,000 more. Say, if you're staying around that long, maybe we could get together again. I mean, I could show the two of you around a little. Are you here alone or with your parents or what?"

Julie answered, "We're with our parents. Thanks for your offer."

"Thanks for accepting it," said Don, although she hadn't said yes or no. The three of them started to laugh, and suddenly Don had that warm feeling of companionship that people usually experience only when they're together with friends whom they've known for a long time.

But it was more than that. When Don sat down in the bus next to Julie, and as he looked to the side at her pretty face and long, black, shiny clean hair lying loosely over her white blouse, and at the innocent smile dimpling her cheeks, he felt very attracted to her. It was not only the ordinary stirring, but something gentle and deep. *Wow!* he thought. *This girl can really pour it on, and probably without even trying.*

2

Weird Neighbor

When Don climbed onto the diving board at the Como Park outdoor swimming pool, Pete looked a little worried. It probably seemed to him that it took a great deal of daring to leap out into space from that altitude. But to Don, standing high above the gently lapping turquoise water of the pool, it was a time of pleasant relaxation; he wasn't even thinking much about the dive he'd be making in a few seconds.

His mind was on Julie. She hadn't come along to the pool because a doctor had warned her to give up swimming for a time. The cut on her arm had become slightly infected but was now improving.

A whole week had passed since Don had met the Canadians, and it had been a good, interesting week. Don had shown Pete and Julie many of the Twin Cities' attractions, including Como Park, Minnehaha Falls, the Nicollet Mall, the International Airport, Fort Snelling, and the Minnesota State Capitol build-

ing with its gold-colored horse statues up near the
dome. He had also taken Pete and Julie into the obser-
vation gallery of the IDS Tower, where from an altitude of 717 feet they had looked out over a shrunken
Minneapolis to a misty horizon more than thirty-five
miles away.

And today the Simmonses were going to start on
their trip back to Canada. This was the part Don didn't
like to think about. He was surprised at how much
Julie had come to mean to him in just a week's time, so
that the thought of her being a thousand miles away
within another day and a half left him feeling dis-
turbed. He knew he would miss Pete too, but the
prospect of being separated permanently from Julie
actually frightened him. He wondered how she felt
about their friendship.

Don also liked Pete and Julie's parents. They were
committed Christians who obviously lived their faith
daily; there seemed to be love and understanding in
every word they spoke and every move they made.
Don loved his own parents, but he wished they were
more like the Simmonses in the matter of definitely
expressing faith in Christ.

Don and the Canadian teenagers had gotten their
parents together near the beginning of the week. The
two families, which included Don's fourteen-year-
old sister, Margie, had spent an evening on the beach
at Lake of the Isles, one of the many lakes within
Minneapolis. And the next evening the Shields had
invited the Simmonses over for dinner. There was

some talk about going to church together on Sunday,
but Mr. Simmons felt it was important to get started
for home by Saturday noon. He said it would be time
to begin haying by Monday, and he wanted to get this
done while the dry weather lasted. Don's father, who
was the manager of a large grocery store, said he
understood, for when he was a young man he had
worked on farms and knew how necessary it was for
farmers to take advantage of suitable weather.

Don bounced up off the springboard and went into
a perfect jackknife, touching his toes before kicking
his legs up. When he hit the water, fingertips first, his
body was straight as a spear, and like a spear he slid
down into the blue depth with hardly a splash. He
leveled off close to the bottom, then glided up slowly
at a shallow angle. Near the surface he did a few
underwater somersaults, then came up in the middle
of a group of swimmers and stroked to the edge of the
pool where Pete was sitting with his feet dangling in
the water. Don hoisted himself up and sat beside the
muscular Canadian.

Pete said, "Man, you sure can swim! You must
spend a lot of time in the water."

"Yeah, I do. You *have* to spend a lot of time in the
water to get your lifeguard certificate and to be able to
pass the periodic tests." Don realized he was bragging
a little, but it always felt good to have someone recognize his swimming ability. To try to make up for the
bragging, he complimented Pete. "Y'know, your
swimming has been improving even in the few days

I've known you. You're better today than you were at
the lake. Especially your sidestroke has improved
since I showed you how to do it right." Don caught
himself working the compliment into self-praise and
decided to change the subject, but Pete looked
pleased.

"Thanks. I sure would like to be able to swim like
you."

"Well," said Don, "my training is coming in handy
now. I get a chance to be of some use at the mental
hospital."

"That's great. Say, do you ever get a chance to talk
to the patients about Christ?"

"Sure."

"Are they bright enough to be able to discuss the
matter like anyone else?"

"Oh sure," said Don. "To see them there, taking
swimming lessons, you wouldn't think there was
anything wrong with them. They talk sensibly, laugh,
and poke fun at one another just like any normal
group of men would do. Last Saturday one of them
sneaked up behind another guy and shoved him into
the deep end. But he could swim, so it was all right.
When he bobbed up he shook his finger at the guy
who had shoved him and told him, 'What's wrong
with you, man? Are you mentally ill?' That sure made
all the others laugh, because they all know why
they're in there."

"If they're like that—I mean if they behave nor-
mally a good deal of the time," began Pete with a

thoughtful look, "isn't it possible that there are a lot of mentally ill people walking the streets? Maybe more than anyone would think?"

"Oh sure," said Don. "I've been studying mental illness on my own by taking books out of the library, because I thought it might help me at the institution if I knew more about it. According to what I read, there are far more mental cases going untreated than those who find their way into hospitals."

"Yeah? Y'know, we have a neighbor living about a mile and a half from our farm. I think he must have something wrong with his mind."

"Oh?" Don vaguely remembered something Julie had said when he had met them at the bus stop. "Didn't Julie mention that you had come on this trip to get away from a mentally ill person? Is he the one you're talking about now?"

"That's right," said Pete, holding up his arm to shield himself from water coming from where some kids were splashing each other. "It wasn't quite like Julie made it sound though. And yet, in a way I guess it was. At first Julie and I weren't sure if we were going to go along on this trip. We thought we might stay home and run the farm while Mom and Dad came down here alone to visit Uncle Ted and Aunt Margaret. But because of this neighbor, Mom and Dad didn't want us to stay home alone. I know it sounds silly because, after all, I'm not exactly a kid anymore, but you know how parents are. And they were especially worried because I'd just had a round of heavy trouble with Ogdeen."

"Ogdeen? Is that the guy's name?"

"Yeah. Anthony Ogdeen. And let me tell you, he's a strange one."

"What kind of trouble did you have with him?"

"Well, in a way it was my fault," said Pete. "But with any other neighbor it wouldn't have turned out like it did. But Ogdeen has trouble with everyone he meets because he hates everyone. He came to Canada about two years ago from Los Angeles, and he didn't make any secret of his reason for leaving that city. You know what it was? He said he was running away from the fools there. He said they were all fools. Nearly everybody he had known since he was a kid, including his father and mother, were fools. That's the way he talked.

"When he got to Saskatchewan, he bought this old deserted farmstead close to where we live and moved in there. At first he was kind of friendly to everyone around, but that didn't last long. He soon made it pretty clear that he thinks all of us, the farmers and those who live in town, are fools too—maybe even bigger fools than the ones he left behind. Now it's gotten to the point where he doesn't try to mix with anyone anymore.

"Of course he has to talk to people sometimes, like when he goes to town to buy groceries, but usually when he does that he gets into a scrap with someone. You wouldn't believe the nasty temper he has! And he's got a tongue like a rawhide whip! Well, I guess several people around there, including me, have found that out from firsthand experience."

"Sounds like some kind of a wild man," put in Don. "What does he do for a living?"

"I don't know. But he paints pictures, so maybe he earns money that way somehow, although I don't see how he could."

"Why not? Some artists make lots of money."

One of the lifeguards, a tall blonde girl, walked by and said hi to Don. He returned the greeting and quickly gave his attention back to Pete, for he found the Canadian's discourse about this weird character, Anthony Ogdeen, definitely interesting.

Pete was saying, "Who would want to buy the kind of paintings he makes? Well, actually I haven't seen any of them myself, but some of the people in town have. At first, when he was still trying to be friendly, he brought some of his paintings in to show them to people in the store; I guess he wanted to put them up on display. Well, Phil Labreque, the store owner, said the pictures were the ugliest things he had ever seen in his life. All sorts of weird garbage, like horrible monsters tearing each other to pieces, or pictures of dead people, and I don't know what else. Philip was careful not to insult Ogdeen, but he sure wasn't going to have those paintings hanging in his store. He told him so, and then Ogdeen got mad and cussed out Phil before he left, fortunately taking his paintings with him."

"Wow! He *is* a weird one!" said Don. "But what about your own trouble with him?"

"Oh, yeah," remembered Pete. "Well, my run-in with him had to do with his paintings too. Julie and I each had a 4-H calf which we were grooming and training for the cattle show we have every summer. That was last year. I don't have any animal to enter this year because I figure I'm getting a little too old for it and should give a chance to the younger kids. Julie will be in it again this year. But anyhow, I had this beautiful Hereford last summer, and I had him well trained too, except for one thing. He was a fence-breaker.

"Well, one part of our corral isn't too good—it's just a gate made of barbed wire—and my steer kept crawling through there and I'd have to go round him up and bring him back. It so happened that one time he strayed over to Ogdeen's place. Ogdeen had been painting outside, and he had left his easel with a half-finished picture on it. When he came out of the house to go back to work on it, there was my steer. He had knocked down the easel and was walking all over the painting. I guess he ruined it completely, so Mr. Ogdeen was really hopping mad.

"To this day I feel lucky to be alive. Ogdeen came over to our place to tell me about it because he knew it was my steer; I had been showing him off in the village one day when Ogdeen was there. So Ogdeen came over and gave me a tongue-lashing like you wouldn't believe, and he warned me never to let my steer get anywhere near his property again. I offered to pay him for the damage, but he wouldn't accept that—said the artwork that had been destroyed was priceless. But anyhow, I apologized and promised to keep my steer off his property.

"The only trouble was that my steer didn't promise too. Four days later he broke out again and headed for Ogdeen's place; I guess he had found pretty good grazing over there. As soon as I realized what had happened, I went straight over to Mr. Ogdeen and asked him if he had seen my steer. He wouldn't talk to me. Slammed the door in my face. I went looking for the animal on his property anyhow, but I couldn't find him there.

"There's a creek that circles around Ogdeen's yard and runs across another neighbor's pasture, so I followed the creek. A ways from where Ogdeen's property comes to an end, there's a beaver dam. That's where I found my steer, close to the water beside the dam and partly covered with brush and trees that the beavers had cut and left lying around. I mean the steer was dead. His head was so bruised that it looked to me as if he had been beaten to death, maybe with a sledgehammer. I know Ogdeen did it."

"Did you report it to the police?" asked Don.

"Yeah, but they couldn't prove anything. And anyhow, the sergeant who investigated the matter said he figured the steer had fallen down the creek bank and had gotten killed by hitting his head against a rock. There was a rock nearby. And then he thought the steer had been kicking around as it died and in that way had managed to get all those trees and brush over itself."

Don rubbed his chin as he thought about it. "The sergeant's theory sounds very unlikely to me."

"It does to me too," said Pete, "but Dad and I decided to let the matter go. Well, things cooled down between Mr. Ogdeen and me; I mean, he didn't get a chance to cuss me out or anything because I think I was avoiding him a little and he may have been avoiding me too. Of course, he stays to himself an awful lot now, so it's not hard to avoid him. But just a couple of weeks ago—a week before we left—I happened to run into him in town, and this time he stopped to talk to me. Well, I don't know if you could call it talking. He told me all over again what he thought of me, and then warned me that this year I was supposed to make sure I kept my animals off his property, and that if I didn't, my steer wouldn't be the only thing that would end up beside the creek. That's what he actually said."

"He was threatening to murder you!"

"Right. But there was no one around besides myself to hear what he said. I don't know if he's actually crazy enough to murder anyone—he may have said that only to scare me—but it made my skin crawl all the same. Now, from what I've told you, what do you think of Mr. Ogdeen?"

Don rubbed his chin some more. "Well, he's obviously in bad shape. And don't be too sure he wouldn't

murder someone. To me he sounds like a classic ex-
ample of a psychopathic personality. I'd say he needs
help, and the sooner the better."

"Maybe you're right," said Pete, looking worried.
He didn't look like himself, for he was usually smiling and talking about cheerful things. "The people
around where I live, including my mom and dad, just
aren't the kind to want to turn anyone over to a mental
institution. I guess they're just sort of old-fashioned
about stuff like that."

"Yeah, well, it's hard to know what to do in a case
like that anyhow," said Don. "I could be wrong. But
by the way you've described him, he sounds like a
dangerous man to have on the loose."

"Hey!" said Pete. "I'd better be getting back. Mom
and Dad will be just about ready to start back to
Canada."

"Yeah," said Don as the two got to their feet. "You
can't miss your ride. Mr. Ogdeen may be getting
lonely for you." Don laughed, but Pete didn't even
smile.

They took a bus to Columbia Heights where Mr.
Simmons had his camping trailer parked in his
uncle's backyard. Ted Simmons and his wife, Margaret, were Pete and Julie's great-uncle and great-
aunt.

Pete's mom and dad, and Julie, were busy getting
the camping trailer ready for the trip when Pete and
Don got there. The boys were in time to help lower the
canvas top and fasten down the wooden cover so that

the trailer became a low, flat conveyance with very little wind resistance.

Don kept looking at Julie, and the disturbing feeling inside him grew until it felt like something had to burst. She was as cute as always. Today she was wearing a white sports outfit as she hopped about nimbly, running back and forth between the house and the car as she helped pack things into the trunk. But now and then he got a good look at her face, and each time he became more convinced that the girl wasn't her usual happy self.

Don began to seriously consider the possibility that Julie was as upset about leaving him as he was about losing her companionship. At first the idea seemed ridiculous, but the more Don looked at Julie the more he became convinced that she was crying inside —crying for him! It was almost like some sort of sixth-sense feeling was passing between them.

Soon everything was packed and the Simmons family stood in a group beside their car with Uncle Ted and Aunt Margaret. Because he wasn't family, Don thought it better to stand off by himself a bit. When the good-byes had been pretty well taken care of, Pete came over and laid his hand on Don's shoulder.

Pete said, "Y'know, it sure would be nice if you could see your way clear to come to Saskatchewan and visit us and stay with us on the farm for a while this summer. I've talked to Mom and Dad about it, and they think that'd be great. I know you can't come now because of your commitment at the institution, but when you get through with your present class of swimmers, maybe you could take a break. Come out to our farm and stay there for a month or so. You can stay all summer if you like; we might even put you to work pitching hay bales or something." He laughed.

Mr. Simmons came walking over. "Don't scare him away," he said. "Don't tell him about the work till after we get him there."

They all laughed about this, even Uncle Ted and Aunt Margaret. Pete's dad was a large, beefy man with a low voice. "Seriously, Don," he said, "we'd be glad to have you come 'round an' spend some time with us, an' I know the kids are sure hopin' you will. So if your dad is still plannin' that trip to Edmonton to take in the managers' conference he was tellin' us about, you tell him he could just as well come through Saskatchewan as go 'round through northern Montana like he is plannin' to. He could drop you off at our place. And we may be makin' another trip back here in the fall, so if that happens you won't even have to spend any money for the trip—goin' or comin'. Well, what do y' say? Should we be lookin' for you?"

Don's eyes slid past Mr. Simmons and Pete and clasped with those of Julie. She was smiling slightly and delicately, almost as if she were afraid to get her hopes up too high. It was a strange and beautiful moment, for they had never looked into each other's eyes like that before in all the friendly, happy times they had spent together during the past week. For several seconds their eyes held, and then Julie looked down shyly at the ground.

Don told Mr. Simmons, "Thank you very much for your offer. I'll do my best to talk Dad into going through Saskatchewan, so you can be expecting me."

3

Ogdeen's Fury

To Pete and Julie the evening chores were something they just took for granted as a part of everyday life, but for Don they were an exciting adventure. There was always some interesting new thing to see and learn about. Not only the chores, but everything on the farm was like that.

Pete, going into the barn with Don, said, "You can help Julie with the milking tonight. She's in a hurry to get to a 4-H Club meeting in town. I'll feed the pigs by myself."

"O.K.," said Don.

Pete walked away toward a doorway that led into the hog section of the barn, and Don turned aside into the separator room where all the milking equipment was kept. It was a large, clean-looking room which contained, among other things, a cream separator, a bucket-type milker, and a large wall refrigerator for milk and medical supplies. There was also an assort-

ment of pails, and on a metal stand was the electric
vacuum pump which ran the milking machine. Don
didn't know where to begin, but he expected Julie to
show up in a few seconds and then they could get
started. He was glad that he'd have another opportunity to be alone with her so they could really talk
and get to know each other better.

Only four days had passed since Don's dad had
dropped him off at the Simmons farm and gone on
alone toward Edmonton and the international conference of store managers, a workshop at which ideas on
efficiency and better service to customers were to be
discussed. Don knew that his dad would stop in on
his way back in about a week and a half, and then he'd
have a chance to return with him to Minneapolis; but
he had already made up his mind to stay on the farm
for the rest of his summer vacation.

It wasn't going to be exactly a vacation though; Don
had found out that much already. He wouldn't have
had to help with any of the farm work, but since he
made it clear that he wanted to, and since Mr. Simmons quickly realized that he was a very energetic
and willing worker, he was offered regular wages.
Don refused this, saying he was being well paid in
hospitality and experience. Mr. Simmons smiled and
said, "We'll see." And that's how the matter stood.

Don heard the outer door of the barn slam and a few
seconds later Julie was hurrying into the separator
room. She was wearing her chore clothes—jeans and
blouse—and had her long dark hair fastened behind

her neck somehow to keep it out of the way while she worked.

"Sorry to make you wait," she said. "Where's Pete?"

"Feeding the pigs. He said he'd do that by himself tonight, and I'm supposed to help you with the milking."

"I know," she said. "I just want to ask him which vehicle I should use when I go to town. Mom and Dad took off with the car—went to a special prayer meeting." She turned to the door and Don saw that a blue ribbon was holding her hair. The long, wavy ponytail swung sharply as she looked back over her shoulder. "You can start giving the cows their chop, if you like," she said.

Don followed her out where two Holsteins and three brindles already stood in their stanchions, waiting to be milked. Pete had brought them in earlier. Don picked up an old battered five-gallon pail and headed for the chop bin which was at the far end of the walking space behind the manger. He filled the pail with a coarsely ground mixture of oats and barley and took it to the cows, where he divided it among them.

Julie returned, and Don followed her back into the separator room. He brought the milking machine out to the cows while Julie prepared a small pailful of soapy water with iodine disinfectant in it. This was for washing the cows' udders. Next she showed Don how to hang the milker on a surcingle strap which

went over the cow's back. Don felt clumsy, for although he had watched Pete and Julie milking, he
hadn't touched any of the equipment himself; his had
been the more unskilled labor of feeding the cows and
pigs.

As Julie made final adjustments on the milker
which now hung underneath the first Holstein to be
milked, Don was already laying another surcingle
over the back of the next cow in line. He thought Julie
looked extra happy tonight and wondered if it was
because she was anticipating the 4-H Club meeting.
This possibility, which seemed sensible enough,
gave Don a feeling of jealousy. He knew it was
ridiculous, but he couldn't help wishing that Julie
would want to stay with him rather than go to the
meeting. Maybe there was a boy there—one of the
other 4-H members—that Julie was hoping to see;
maybe that's why she looked excited.

Don was amazed at himself. Never before had he
gotten so keyed up over a girl. To get his mind off
what he considered to be silly thoughts, he decided to
talk to Julie about something really important. It
bothered Don that during the four days he had been
here on the farm, he and Julie hadn't once discussed
spiritual matters.

"I hope your mom and dad and everyone else at
church tonight has—I mean, I hope they have a good
prayer meeting." Don's tongue fumbled with words
as his fingers fumbled with a metal rod connected to
the surcingle. He finally got it stuck through the

proper hole so that it hung under the cow at the right
height for the milker to be suspended from it.

Julie just smiled at him as she stood beside the other
Holstein and stroked its back. White liquid was already spurting through the milking machine's clear
plastic tubes.

He tried again. "Don't you think it would be a good
idea if you and Pete and I could get together for a few
minutes sometimes and have a kind of little prayer
meeting of our own?" Don had been thinking about
this possibility for a couple of days.

But Julie didn't seem to get very excited about it.
"Well, we pray together with Mom and Dad every
day, you know. And usually we go to the prayer
meetings in church too. But tonight I have the 4-H
meeting, and Mom and Dad agreed that it was my
responsibility to go to that. As for Pete, he has to stay
home because there's a cow about to freshen—the one
in the box stall. She could have her calf any moment,
and someone has to stay around."

"How come they have the 4-H meeting on the same
night that there's a prayer meeting?"

"They don't usually do that," said Julie. "It was a
mix-up. Our regular prayer meeting is tomorrow. But
the pastor called one for tonight too because there's a
missionary from Kenya visiting him today, so
everyone's going to pray for the mission work there.
And they're holding the meeting an hour earlier than
usual because the missionary has another speaking
engagement tonight somewhere else. The 4-H meet-

ing could have been canceled but we have a special
speaker tonight too, all the way from Calgary. He's
going to give us some kind of lecture on beef cattle. I
don't really know what it's going to be about, but it'll
probably be pretty interesting, at least if you like
cattle as I do." And she went on like that, talking
about previous speakers and about cattle shows that
had been held in town.

During the rest of the milking Don gave up trying to
swing the conversation toward spiritual matters. He
supposed it was good that Julie had this keen interest
in cattle. And he seemed to recall hearing or reading
that the 4-H Club had been founded on Christian
principles.

They were all done with milking, separating, and
washing the equipment before Don got up enough
nerve to ask Julie if he could ride along to town with
her. Again he felt silly because ordinarily he could
have asked a girl something like that without thinking twice about it.

"Sure, Don." She smiled. "Why not come along to
the meeting? They wouldn't mind."

He opened the barn door for her and they walked
out onto the yard which was bathed in the gold-red
haze of a low sun shining through thin clouds.

"No, I'd feel out of place. I can explore your big city
while you're at the meeting."

They both laughed about this, because the "big
city" which was usually referred to as the "town" was
really too small to even be truthfully honored with the

title of "village." Its population amounted to about seventy-five. But it had a fair-sized church, and its single general store did a brisk business with rural customers from a large surrounding area.

By hurrying very much, Don and Julie got cleaned up and ready to leave in just a little over half an hour. Julie looked really sharp in a dark blue jumper and a red and white candy-striped blouse. Her long black hair was spread out over her shoulders. Don felt a little crude in comparison as they walked out toward the pickup, for he hadn't gone further than to put on a clean outfit of faded blue denim.

"You drive, O.K.?" said Julie.

"Sure." Don had already driven the old half-ton pickup and liked it. In a way it was more fun than driving his dad's Oldsmobile or his own car which he had bought last year and had run two months before the motor conked out. Until now he had never had the opportunity to drive a pickup.

It felt good to have Julie sitting beside him as he guided the pickup down the long lane and turned onto the high gravel road that led to the village two miles away. This was almost like having a date with her. Maybe it was a date.

They met Mr. and Mrs. Simmons coming home from church and stopped on the road for a few minutes to talk. Both of Julie's parents looked quite undisturbed about seeing Don and Julie driving away alone together, and although Don hadn't really expected any other reaction, he felt relieved. It was only after he had already asked Julie if he could ride to town with her that he had thought of the possibility that maybe she needed her parents' permission for this sort of thing. Everything was all right though, and the two vehicles carried on in their opposite directions.

It made Don feel good to know that Julie's parents trusted him. Why did they? They certainly hadn't known him very long. Don supposed it was mainly because they knew he was a follower of Christ.

"I really like your parents, Julie, and I sure am glad they're Christians. Y'know, you and Pete are lucky to have parents who are surrendered to God, who can teach you really good things. I know they do. I'm learning from them too."

"Aren't your parents Christians?" asked Julie.

"I'm not sure," Don said. "I think Mom is, but she doesn't say much about it. Dad goes to church too, and I think he would call himself a Christian. But if he's really had the second-birth experience, you'd think he'd say something about it. I love my parents, and they've been very good to me. They've done so much for me I'll never be able to thank them enough. I pray for them a lot, and someday I hope they'll put their full trust in Christ, if they haven't yet."

"Mom and Dad have been good to me too," said Julie.

Don asked, "Do you and Pete have a chance to get together with Christians your own age?"

"Not much; there aren't many around here." Julie

flicked on the radio. There was a newscast on, but she punched the tuning buttons until she found some rock music. "By the way," she said, "did Dad tell you that he wants you to ride out to the community pasture tomorrow? You know, the place where we took you for a ride the first day you were here. He wants you to go check on our cattle, to count them and see if they all look all right. It's not hard to tell them from the rest, because they're the only Charolais there. But one of the riders over there will probably help you anyhow. You don't have to go if you don't want to, but I guess Dad thought you might enjoy a day in the saddle. You seemed to dig riding Pete's horse the other day."

"I sure did," said Don, "and I'll be glad to go. I've done a bit of trail riding. I went to a Bible camp one summer where they had horses. That was a good summer; we sure had a lot of fun. But what was more important, we learned some cool things out of the Bible."

"That's good," said Julie, turning the radio volume up a little higher. "Were the horses pretty lively, or did you have to be content with riding a bunch of old crowbaits?"

"Oh no, they were nice Arabians," said Don. And so they continued to talk about horses as they turned into the main street of the village.

The sun was setting now, and there was light already in the general store. When Don asked if this was a late shopping night, Julie laughed and explained that Phil Labreque's store had late shopping every night, even Sundays. In fact, it was pretty hard to catch the place closed. Labreque more or less lived there behind his cash register, either serving customers or playing solitaire, as the occasion demanded.

"Hey, where's your meeting?" said Don. "I forgot to ask."

"It's in that house right next to the store, on this side of it. The president of the club lives there."

"I guess I'll go in the store for a while."

"The cafe is just around the corner. It's open too." Julie reached for the door handle as she prepared to step out. But then she sat motionless, staring straight ahead.

Don swung his face toward the general store to see what had attracted her attention. Two men stood there, talking. The one facing the truck was small and delicately built and wore a dark suit with a white shirt and necktie. A few seconds earlier Don had seen him approaching along the sidewalk. The other man, his back toward the truck, had probably just come out of the store. He was huge—tall and fat—and his bright red sport shirt didn't help to make him look any smaller.

"Now this is something really interesting," said Julie.

"Oh?"

"That's Pastor Unger talking to Mr. Ogdeen."

Don had suspected that the big man was Anthony Ogdeen, for both Pete and Julie had described his physical appearance and had told Don several more ugly stories about this strange man who lived only a mile and a half on the other side of the farm. And here he was in conversation with the village pastor who had just come away from the evening's prayer meeting. It was the drama of an encounter between good and evil that had captivated Julie's attention, and Don felt the same need to sit still and watch.

It turned out to be more dramatic than the two teenagers expected. At first they couldn't hear any words, but in a few seconds Mr. Ogdeen began to wave his arms around in a way that showed he was becoming emotionally agitated, and at this point his voice rose so that a few words came through distinctly. He was cursing the other man.

Now the pastor was speaking again. A look of gentleness and entreaty was on his thin face. His hands were slightly raised with the palms up in a gesture of pleading.

Then Mr. Ogdeen walked forward, probably to go to a car parked a few yards up the street, but he didn't bother to make a detour around the man in front of him. Pastor Unger tried to step aside to avoid being walked over, but he didn't quite make it. The men's bodies came in contact, and the pastor stumbled backward. Mr. Ogdeen swung out a big arm, and with something that was halfway between a push and a blow sent the smaller man reeling so that he no longer could keep his balance. He fell to the cement with his head and shoulders banging against the storefront. Ogdeen didn't even look back as he moved on toward his vehicle.

Don was out of the truck in half a second. As he reached Pastor Unger, a tall, thin man came out of the store and in an excited voice asked what was going on. Don told him what he had seen as they knelt beside the downed man. A moment later Julie joined them.

The pastor wasn't unconscious, only groggy. He pushed himself up a little higher and sat leaning against the wall. Then he shook his head slowly, either to clear the fog out of it or as a gesture of sadness about what had happened. Ogdeen's car roared away down the street and disappeared around a corner.

The tall man addressed the pastor by his first name. "Sam," he said, "did that—that big ape hit you?"

Sam felt the back of his head. "No—no, he just pushed me a little. I stumbled and fell and hit my head against the wall. I'm all right."

"I'm just about fed up with that guy," said the other man. "I've got half a mind to go beat the tar out of him! I'll teach him to shove people around. Right in front of my store too, as if he owns the place. Next thing you know he'll be throwin' my customers out through the front door!"

Pastor Sam Unger began to get to his feet, so Don and the store owner helped him, one on each side. Sam said, "Take it easy, Phil. It wouldn't help any to beat up on him. What he needs is to have people praying for him. And don't make too big a thing out of what happened here. He didn't hit me. I was in his way, and he became annoyed and pushed me. He was very upset and wasn't fully aware of what he was doing."

Phil asked, "What was he so mad about?"

"I don't know," said the pastor. "I was talking to him about the love of God."

*　　　*　　　*

Later, after the 4-H meeting was over and Don and Julie were driving back to the farm, Don told her, "I think something should be done about Mr. Ogdeen. The police should be called in."

"Maybe," said Julie, "but it's not likely to happen."

"Why not? I don't agree with the pastor that all that needs to be done is to pray for the man. I think the Christian thing to do in a case like this is to notify the police and have them investigate Mr. Ogdeen. So if the people around here are Christians, I think that's what they *will* do."

Julie said, "Have you ever heard of hypocrites?"

4

Cloudburst

The thunderstorm came up quickly, for a northwest wind was trundling the bulky, rain-laden clouds across the open countryside at a furious speed.

Don, alone on horseback, was returning from his errand of checking Mr. Simmons's cattle at the community pasture. He had seen the storm coming like a great dark curtain stretching from one side of the horizon to the other and growing larger rapidly. It had frightened him just a little, for he was a city boy, and in a city, with its man-made skyline, one seldom sees that sort of awesome spectacle in its entirety.

Now the storm was here, blackening the early evening sky and then rending that blackness with crooked forks of electric light, and hurling gallons of cold water at Don and the horse he rode. The youth realized that this was no ordinary thunderstorm but something more like a cloudburst. And the center of the electrical activity was now directly overhead so

that lightning and thunder broke loose simultaneously. Don was aware of the danger; his apprehension
grew as the lightning increased its frequency and as
his horse began to stumble a bit in the muddy water
that filled deep ruts on the gravel road at one low
point.

"Come on, Pedro." He tried to encourage the bay
quarter horse, but a roar of wind, water, and thunder
swept away all lesser sounds, including Don's voice.
Through driving sheets of rain he could just barely
make out the tall poplar trees beside the road; they
were leaning with the storm, swaying and bobbing.

Don knew there was shelter available nearby, but
he was very reluctant to make use of it. He could see
the place—the towering old pines that stood sentinel
all around the yard—immediately to his left. Yes,
there was the lane, but it looked more like a canal
now. Water from higher ground was flooding the
whole yard of Anthony Ogdeen.

Don pulled Pedro to a stop at the open gateway,
knowing that under ordinary circumstances he
would hurry to the man's door and ask for shelter. But
he remembered all that Pete had told him about this
strange neighbor, plus what he himself had seen yesterday in the village, and something close to outright
fear held him back. Pedro didn't feel like going into
the yard either, but his reason was simply that he
wanted to get on home to his cozy stall at the Simmons farm. That was only another mile and a half
distant.

Don mulled over the matter during the few seconds
that he held his horse back from carrying on toward
home. Lightning, wind, and rain continued in full
intensity. *Maybe the horse is right,* thought Don.
*Maybe it would be better to try to get to Simmons's
farm and just forget about immediate shelter and
Anthony Ogdeen.*

For ten more long seconds Don sat still in the saddle, his wet jacket collar turned up and the streaming
brim of his hat pulled down. Then, suddenly, he
neck-reined Pedro into the lane that led toward the
old two-story house where Ogdeen lived all alone. *If
he's really in as bad a shape as they say,* thought Don,
*then it's time everybody really started to take an
interest in him to see what can be done to help him.*

The lane was very nearly impassable, even on
horseback. In places Pedro had to pick his way carefully through washouts and ankle-deep streams of
fast-running water. Once they were on the yard, progress became a little easier, for the ground was higher
toward the house. But Don noticed with alarm that in
several places wide streams of water were literally
tearing out strips of the soil. It was obvious that if this
flooding should continue for even an hour, there
would be nothing left of Ogdeen's yard. Getting off
the place might be more difficult than getting on.

Don rode uphill until he was very close to an unpainted door leading into an unpainted porch.
Farther along the side of the old house, bright light
outlined curtained windows.

Don dismounted and rapped on the door. There was no response the first time, but soon after his second knock the door opened away from his fist and revealed the silhouetted outline of Ogdeen's bulky, bearlike form. Ogdeen was fat, but he was also tall and his chest was wide. His head was small in comparison with the rest of his body, but it looked large because of a shaggy mane of hair. Don couldn't yet see a face clearly in the silhouette, but somehow he knew the man's expression was unfriendly. The silhouette stood completely motionless.

Don yelled over the roar of the storm, "Hello! My name's Don Shield. I stay at the Simmonses' place. I was riding home from the community pasture when this storm came up. Can I come inside for a while till it blows over?"

The bulky outline remained motionless and silent as several seconds passed. Then a great flash of lightning changed the silhouette into a three-dimensional form. For two seconds Don could see the face clearly. Its expression was worse than he had imagined. It was a study in hatred—out-and-out hatred. *But why?* thought Don. *What have I ever done to make this complete stranger hate me?* Then Don remembered that people said Anthony Ogdeen hated everyone.

As the thunder died away, Ogdeen finally spoke. "All right. Put your horse in the barn and come in the house."

Almost shocked by these words, Don replied, "Yes, sir," and at once turned back to his horse. He mounted and rode over the rapidly deteriorating yard toward a dilapidated-looking hip-roofed barn that probably hadn't been used for years. There was no light inside, so Don groped his way into the nearest stall. He tied Pedro's bridle reins to the manger, then unsaddled him.

It took some time to find a safe place to put the saddle and blanket so rats wouldn't get at them. His first blind try was the stall partition, but it turned out to be mostly missing and broken down. But at the gutter there was an upright beam with a harness-hanging peg protruding from it. Don hung the saddle on this peg by one stirrup and then hung the other stirrup and the girth ring over the saddle horn. He tied the blanket to a leather thong behind the cantle.

The trek back across the yard was tough going, to say the least. By the time Don arrived at the porch, he was plastered with mud higher than the tops of his riding boots. The rest of his clothing was completely saturated with cold rain water, but it had been that way since the beginning of the storm.

He knocked again.

"Come in!" yelled the angry-sounding voice of Anthony Ogdeen.

Don stepped inside and closed the door, grateful for the sudden comparative quiet. As he turned away from the door, he prayed silently: *Dear God, please help me to make the best of whatever this is I've gotten myself into.* He walked through an open doorway into what must originally have been a kitchen, but now it was such a fantastic and dreadful-looking place that it took all of Don's courage to keep from turning around and fleeing out into the storm.

The room was brightly lit by a double-mantled gas lamp that hung from a smoky ceiling. About in the center of the room was a wooden table at which sat Ogdeen with an artist's brush in one hand and a paint-speckled palette in the other. A partly finished canvas was propped up by hooks on the table in front of him. This painting, plus a great many others that covered almost every square inch of wall in the room, depicted in bright colors scenes so gruesome that Don's flesh tightened into goose pimples. Without a single exception, the pictures showed people being executed in a great variety of horrible ways. Some were being stabbed, some were being shot, some were being brutally clubbed to death, and so on.

Ogdeen waited until Don had finished his brief survey of the paintings. Then the bulky man put down his brush and waved a huge hand in a gesture that indicated the cruel paintings.

"Something like that," said Ogdeen, "is what should happen to all fools!"

5

The Maniac

"Have a chair," said Mr. Ogdeen.

Don pulled his eyes away from the fiendishly cruel paintings and noticed for the first time that there was other furniture in the room in addition to the table at the side of which Ogdeen sat. There was a wooden bench along one wall, several chairs along another, and something that might have been a coffee table next to Ogdeen's chair. On this low table was an assortment of paint tubes, pencils, charcoal sticks, a bottle marked "turpentine," and various other art supplies.

Don looked down at his muddy feet, then began to take off his boots. "Thank you. I'll have to get out of these before I go any farther, and I guess my clothes are so wet I'll be dripping all over everything."

"That can't be helped," returned Ogdeen sternly. He now sat with his fingers laced under his chin, propping up his head with his elbows on the table. In dark pants and solid-black turtleneck sweater, and

56

with his shaggy black hair framing a round, heavy-featured face, he seemed to be a thundercloud personfied—a very bulky thundercloud.

Don had his boots off. He held his dripping hat in his hand, looking for a place to put it. The porch was the obvious answer, so he took the boots and hat there and also removed his jacket. He tried to press some of the water out of his blue jeans and blue denim shirt before reentering the studio. When he did walk back into the brightly lit room, Ogdeen was up on his feet.

"Come into the other room," invited the bulky man. "I've got a fire going in the heater. You need to dry out a bit."

"Thanks," said Don as he followed Ogdeen into a larger chamber that was lit only by the transparent mica front of an oil heater. In the gloom a variety of rectangular forms suggested living room furniture.

"Get close to the stove," said Ogdeen. "I'll get the lamp." He went back into his studio and in a moment returned holding the gas light which he then hung on a hook in the living room ceiling.

Don almost wished that the room had been left in semidarkness, for the light revealed that one whole wall was a mural depicting a man with his head on a chopping block under a raised ax.

As the boy stood looking at this ugly, larger-than-life rendering, Ogdeen was studying him with equal interest. What he saw was a tall, slim, athletically built youth with an alert face and dark hair that the rain had plastered to his forehead and ears.

Don got his eyes away from the mural and unconsciously began to inspect the rest of the room. Ogdeen said, "You look like an intelligent kid."

It was surely a strange thing to say. Don couldn't think of any response so he kept silent and continued to look about the cubicle, noting that it was a combination of living room, dining room, and bedroom; it had the necessary furniture for all three. *Maybe Ogdeen doesn't use the rest of the house,* thought Don.

The boy moved closer to the oil heater. "This feels good. I'm very grateful."

Ogdeen sat down on a sofa under the gruesome mural. "Don't thank me; it just confuses things."

Don thought that over for a few seconds, then said, "I don't understand. What's confusing about it?"

"It's confusing," said Mr. Ogdeen, "because I didn't let you come in here because of any kindness on my part. My reason for letting you come in out of the storm was strictly selfish."

"Oh? May I ask what that reason was?"

"Of course. Always ask when you want to know something. Don't be like the rest of the fools out there." He waved a fat hand around in a circle that seemed to enclose the entire human race. "As a matter of fact, I had at least two reasons—both of them selfish—for letting you come in here. In the first place, if I let you come to harm in the storm I might be charged with criminal negligence and end up in jail. But my second and more important reason for inviting you in is that I have a natural need for human company, just as everyone has, and for quite some time now I've had very little contact with anyone."

Don bent over the heater, spreading out his fingers and enjoying the physical comfort of warmth seeping into his chilled body. But his mind was far from comfortable. "Why do you stay here all alone so much?" he asked.

"Because," said Ogdeen, and his round face took on a remarkably patient look, "—because it's better to be alone than to be with fools. The people I've become acquainted with around here so far have, without exception, been mental weaklings who contributed absolutely nothing to the conversations I've tried to carry on with them. Oh, I suppose that's a slight exaggeration. There have been a couple or so with whom I've been able to carry on a reasonably interesting conversation, and on occasion they've even come up with some worthwhile homespun philosophy. But as a general rule they've been disappointing."

"I have a feeling you're going to be disappointed in me too. I may be even less intelligent than some of the people you've met around here."

"Don't underestimate yourself, boy. What did you say your name is?"

"Don Shield."

"Don't underestimate yourself, Don. You're still young. You seem to have a bright mind; I can tell. If only you could keep from following the stupidity of the older people who have been trying to teach you wrong things."

Don wondered how old Anthony Ogdeen was, and decided he must be somewhere around forty.

"Older people have tried to teach me *some* wrong things; I don't doubt that," admitted Don. "But some of them have also taught me a lot of good things."

"Maybe you just think they're good things," suggested Ogdeen as he stretched his heavy lips into a smile. The austere expression was gone from his face now, and he looked almost happy; but evil still lived in his dark eyes. "You'll have to make up your mind to stop believing what people tell you, and start using your own head."

"I guess I don't know exactly what you're getting at."

"I'll explain. Sit down and make yourself comfortable. Pull that chair up close to the fire and sit down and relax. We'll have a good talk. If you listen carefully to what I tell you, I might be able to get you started on the right track. By the way, what do you think of my paintings?"

"They're very well done," said Don with honesty as he brought the chair close to the heater. He sat down. "But I can't say the subject matter appeals to me. In fact, it turns me off. Why do you paint so many pictures of people being killed?"

"Wonderful!" exclaimed Ogdeen. "You have enough nerve and individuality to say what you think. Most people hedge around and won't tell me what they really think. I knew I had you sized up right. Now to give an honest answer to your honest

question. I paint the pictures as a scientific, accepta-
ble way of releasing my anger. The victims in my
pictures represent the fools of this world. They are the
many stupid people who are a hindrance to progress
in civilization. In the paintings I do to them what I'd
really like to do to them in real life if opportunity
allowed."

For several seconds the man and boy looked stead-
fastly across the room at each other. Finally Don
spoke. "I feel sorry for you, Mr. Ogdeen. I mean it. I
hope that someday you find true happiness."

"Who says I'm not happy? I'm happy when I think
of murdering people who are fools, and I'm happy
when I'm talking to intelligent persons, sharing my
thoughts with them."

Don said, "You won't be really happy and have
peace in your mind until you get right with God. And
the way to get right with God is through Jesus Christ."

For five seconds Ogdeen made no reply and sat
completely expressionless and motionless. But Don
could see a paleness coming over the man's round
face. Then Ogdeen slowly rose to his feet with his big
hands clenching and unclenching grotesquely at his
sides. "Get out of here!" he yelled. Don realized that
Ogdeen's brief silence had been caused by surprise.
He also knew definitely that he was not dealing with
an entirely sane man. The artist's face was now a
terrible thing to see, it was so distorted by rage. "I
thought you might be somebody I could talk to. But
you're the worst kind—a Christian! If I had known

that, I'd never have invited you in! And now you can
get back out! Get out!"

Don was on his feet, but somehow he could not yet
turn to leave. He said, "Why do you hate Christians so
much?"

Ogdeen took a step forward. "Because they stand in
the way of progress more than anyone else!" he
shouted. "You believe there's a great God who'll take
care of everything for you so that you don't have to do
any thinking yourselves. You're the greatest lot of
fools in the whole world!" He kicked a chair so that it
went crashing across the room, narrowly missing
Don.

For a couple of seconds Don stood rooted to the
floor, shocked by the violence. Some fear must have
shown in his face, and in that moment a change came
over Ogdeen.

The big man looked down at the floor and shook his
shaggy head. "I'm—I'm sorry," he said. "I—have a
bad temper. I don't keep it under control the way I
should."

With some difficulty Don found his voice. "It's all
right."

"You can stay if you want to," said Mr. Ogdeen.

"Thank you, but maybe I'd better go. Maybe
—maybe I'll stop in again some other time." Don felt
guilty about refusing the offer; it was almost like
turning down the apology, and possibly it was giving
up an opportunity to help the man. But Don was not
only a little bit afraid; he was angry and indignant. He

wanted to get out of this house, away from this obviously mentally ill person, this maniac!

Don walked through the studio and onto the porch where he hastily put on his boots, jacket, and hat. When he pressed the outer door latch he was whipped backward by the wind-flung door. He stumbled but kept his balance.

As he crossed the threshold a flash of lightning revealed the yard, or what had been a yard. The highest part near the house was a bog of mud; the lower part surrounding the barn and leading to the lane was completely flooded. In the brief moment that passed as Don stumbled out into the lightning-illuminated storm, he could see fallen trees and smaller driftwood moving along rapidly with the floodwater. A second later he was face down in the mud, for he had slipped on the wet doorstep.

Don struggled to his feet as thunder shook the darkness. He still didn't want to go back into the house or even stay close to it. But how could he hope to get through the surrounding flood? How could he get to his horse or off the yard without being struck by floating trees or being swept away? He guessed correctly that the creek which ran near Ogdeen's buildings was spilling its high water across the yard.

Don plodded forward in ankle-deep mud, heading toward the hazardous floodwater that surrounded the barn.

6

The Flood

Lightning crackled over the Ogdeen farmstead as Don slid downward from ankle-deep mud into knee-deep moving floodwater. He had another thirty feet to go before reaching the barn. Bracing himself against the current, he struggled forward.

The many individual streams cascading down the slope of Ogdeen's yard were pooling in a wide, level area around the barn, so here the flow had lost some of its force. Still, as Don moved into this deeper water, he found the current strong enough to almost pull his feet out from under him. He waded carefully, bracing himself against the flow and doing his best not to trip over anything.

He reached the barn safely and spent the remainder of his strength forcing the door open against mud that had piled up. Then he waited for his muscles to recuperate a little. In a few seconds he was able to go on.

The water inside the old stable was deeper than outside; it reached halfway up Don's thighs. He felt his way through darkness toward the stall where he had tied Pedro.

The horse let out a snort and splashed around in the deep water.

"Easy, boy," soothed Don. "It's only me. I'm glad you're still here." He was also glad the animal was remarkably gentle-natured.

Don quickly found the saddle and threw it on Pedro's back without using the blanket. He fumbled with the cinch for at least sixty seconds before getting it in place free of twists. Then he pulled the leather strap through the cinch ring and tied a saddle knot as Pete had taught him, but this was the first time he had ever done it in complete darkness. He untied the bridle reins from the manger.

"Come on, Pedro; let's get out of here. We have to get home." The horse followed willingly as Don led him to the door; but instead of passing through into the moving flood immediately, Don paused for several seconds while he asked God to help him get safely to the Simmons farm. Then he mounted and, ducking his head low, rode out through the open doorway.

Once more the wind lashed violently at horse and rider. As they splashed forward in the darkness, Don had the feeling that he was riding into deeper water, but there was no lightning just now so he couldn't be sure. He turned Pedro in what he hoped was the right direction. After a moment the horse wanted to angle toward the right-hand side, but Don felt sure the lane was more to the left, so he forced Pedro to turn back that way. It was a big mistake. Don realized this about a minute later when an overdue flash of lightning showed him how far off course he was. Pedro had been right, and Don was angry at himself for not having had enough sense to give the animal a free rein. He remembered reading about how horses can find their way in the dark much better than people.

Don wondered what he should do, for as lightning continued to flash he could see the top of a barbed-wire fence jutting up out of the water ahead of him. He couldn't get to the lane that way now; his only chance was to do a complete about-face and let Pedro retrace his steps almost back to the barn where the fence started. Don realized that he had unknowingly steered his horse through an open gateway that led into a field or pasture.

The current was from the rear and had become very strong. As Don began to turn Pedro, lightning flared brightly and showed a large fallen tree sweeping toward them. It was only thirty or twenty-five feet away.

Don put heels to the horse and slapped him sharply with the loose end of the reins. Pedro leaped forward so quickly that Don lost his balance and slid from the saddle.

He hit the water on his side and went under, but still he held tightly to one bridle rein. Surfacing quickly, Don grabbed the saddle horn. The horse, very excited now, continued to splash forward and pulled Don along like a cork.

The big tree sailed on by, but it passed so closely that one of its sharp, broken branches scraped against Don's boot.

Pedro came to a stop, snorting and trembling. Don quickly managed to get his feet back under him. He wasn't hurt; he hadn't even lost his hat, for it now hung on his shoulders supported by the chin strap. But he was gasping for air as he straightened up still more in the waist-deep water.

"Whoa, Pedro! Whoa!" Somehow he made it back up into the slippery saddle. The gelding walked deeper into the floodwater, away from the lane. Apparently he had given up trying to get home by that route. Now Don attempted nothing but to hang onto the horn with both hands.

When lightning flashed he could see the dangerous driftwood rushing by on all sides. Sometimes he thought Pedro might be swimming; at other times he was almost sure the horse's legs had buckled down into the mud and that all hope of survival was futile. But then he would become aware of the animal's walking motion again and would know once more that they were moving.

The downhill rush of the flood increased its momentum continuously as it pushed Pedro along relentlessly toward lower ground. Don's alarm soared as he guessed that he was being drawn into the flooded creek. A big tree twirled by, narrowly missing the horse; Don had not yet finished breathing his sigh of relief when an even larger one bore down on them

from the side and rear. As if it were a missile accu-
rately hurled by some gigantic underwater demon, it
came straight on toward horse and rider.

Don threw up his leg to avoid having it broken. The
log rammed into Pedro's ribs. Pedro grunted as he
was thrown to the side and forward. Once more Don
left the saddle, rolling backward over the horse's
rump; after the boy's head came up above the water's
surface he found that his feet couldn't reach bottom.

He doubled up at the waist and reached down to
remove his boots, but before he could get a grip on
them a branch of another drifting tree hooked his arm.
It was not a hard contact, for he and the piece of
driftwood were caught in the same eddy and were
moving along at about the same speed. Don grabbed a
hold of the log with both hands and pulled himself up
alongside of it.

A few seconds later, under the fluorescent glare of
lightning, Don could see clearly that he and the log
had been flushed right into the middle of the creek, a
creek that the flood had turned into a raging, boiling,
fifty-foot-wide torrent of white foaming water and
churning driftwood. The flow on the yard had been as
nothing compared to this. Don was a good swimmer
and he knew it, but this didn't prevent him from
hanging onto the big log as though his life depended
on it. Maybe this was the case, for the floating tree not
only gave him support but also protected him consid-
erably from other debris which was bobbing and
prodding on all sides. Don's tree was larger than the

surrounding driftwood, and for the most part the big log floated along parallel with the current.

Don wondered what had become of Pedro but couldn't catch any sight of him even though the rapid lightning offered plenty of bright illumination. Too much driftwood was all around.

Where Don was now, the swollen creek was about fifty feet wide, but it was becoming narrower—that much Don could catch glimpses of as he bobbed up and down beside his torpedolike log—and this meant that the current would be increasing. The danger of being smashed against a rock or torn to pieces by jagged driftwood became greater with every passing second.

Some sort of obstruction was in the water not far ahead. A dam? As he swept rapidly toward it and as the electrical storm gave him a series of bright glimpses, Don quickly realized that he was looking at a beaver dam—or what was left of it. The raging creek had torn a four-foot-wide chunk out of its center and was gushing through at that point with a jetlike pressure that sent white foam spraying even higher than the dam. It was obvious that under that terrible force the remaining parts of the dam would also soon buckle and be washed away. But so far the intertwined branches still stuck up about six inches above the swirling surface of the creek.

Don didn't know if he wanted the side parts of the dam to hold till he got there or not. If they held, then he'd likely be sucked through the center with a lot of crowding driftwood. That in itself could be enough to kill him, but he could also be dashed against a boulder or impaled on a sharp branch. Yet he hated to think of the dam washing away completely—even though that might prolong his life—for this obstruction in the water seemed like his only chance to climb up out of the creek and get to shore. It was a very slim chance.

He was only seventy-five or sixty feet away from the beaver dam. The sounds of current and thunder mixed into one great terrifying roar as an eye-searing, prolonged flash of lightning showed Don that he was being swept directly toward the opening in the dam. Now he could clearly see that there were many sharp, jagged branches sticking up through the rushing water. He was thirty feet away from death and knew it.

But that was also when he suddenly knew what to do. Using all his strength, he twisted at the big log. He was not trying to change its direction, which would have been impossible, but was trying to swing it crosswise on the current. He was lucky; the eddying water near the dam actually helped him a little in his effort. In two seconds he had the log twisted around in front of him so that the ends stuck out to either side. With a jar that was cushioned somewhat by the springy branches of the dam, the long log lodged squarely across the opening.

Don had all he could do to keep the current from sucking him through underneath. His biceps and

chest muscles contracted into steel-hard knots as he
pulled himself upward in an attempt to climb onto
the log, and then he slid back downward as the current began to win. He forced himself upward again,
and higher this time. Now, with his elbows on top, he
was able to raise himself high enough so that he could
drag one knee out of the water and fling it up onto the
log. But that was a mighty effort that almost drained
the remainder of his strength. After a few seconds of
comparative rest, he pulled his other leg up. Then the
tree suddenly began to tremble under his knees. Had
there been continuous darkness he would have fallen,
but the rapidly flashing lightning helped him maintain his precarious perch on the log.

The lightning also showed him that the remainder
of the dam was cracking up; that was why the log was
trembling. Don knew he had to make a move—and a
fast one—to get off this lodged log and the dam before
it was all dashed out from under him. But he was
afraid to let go his grip.

A bolt of bluish lightning cracked and sizzled close
over his head. For a moment he was deaf from the
concussion, but he hardly noticed; his attention was
absorbed by what he had seen during that brief, awful
glare. Another chunk had just been ripped out from
the piece of dam in front of him over which he had
hoped to crawl to safety. And now the tree under him
was shaking violently.

As lightning flashed again, Don let go and sprang to
his feet. Straight forward along the wet log he

leaped—almost flew—knowing deep inside of him
that only a miracle could keep his feet from slipping.
In two jumps and two seconds he was off the log and
felt his boots crunch in among the top twigs of the
beaver dam. He kept right on going, leaping in the
dark over the place where he knew the flood had
ripped out another hole. Lightning flashed only after
he landed on the other side of it, and as he continued
to charge forward he could see this last bit of the dam
breaking up under his feet.

He flung himself toward the bank. Another flash of
lightning showed him an upright tree—a slender
poplar rooted close to the foaming water's edge. Don
let himself fall forward and reached out for the base of
the trunk. As his chest slammed into the muddy bank,
his wrist made contact with the tree's smooth bark. In
a fragment of a second he had grabbed the trunk with
both hands, and that determined grip was enough to
anchor him securely while he felt the remainder of
the beaver dam rip out from under his legs. His face
was half buried in mud and his eyes closed, but he
could hear a splintering of branches even above the
roar of water and wind, and he knew that the dam had
now been swept away entirely.

The water, not held back any longer, dropped several feet as it leveled off. Don found that his legs were
clear of it; the length of his body lay at a steep angle on
the bank.

He was in that position for only a few seconds. His
muscles and nervous system were still in high gear,

and he quickly pulled himself up past the tree to more level ground. But then, once he had reached this place of comparative safety, he collapsed completely.

Don lay there in the grass like a wet rag while the driving rain continued to pound down on him, and the lightning and thunder went on with their clamorous battle in the sky.

7

Second Encounter

"One of these days I'm gonna break down and buy a few raincoats," promised Mr. Simmons after he and Pete had made the quick dash from house to truck. The stocky farmer and his eighteen-year-old son were drenched.

"Raincoats wouldn't help enough for this kind of rain," Pete said as he tried to wring water out of his sleeves by rolling them up over his muscular arms. "Skin-diving outfits would be more practical."

Mr. Simmons guided the half-ton pickup down their muddy lane and onto the high-graded road. He said, "Don prob'ly found shelter somewhere, but I'd drive faster if I could."

At fifty-one Arthur Simmons was in good physical shape except that he carried a little too much weight. But he was solid and strong. His mind was like his body—solid, sound, full of a simple wisdom not gained from books. His father had been a homesteader

74

in a northern area of Saskatchewan that had still been close to the pioneer stage and where schooling had not seemed very important to anyone, so Arthur Simmons hadn't made it past fourth grade. He had dropped out of school so that he could help his dad with the farm work.

Like others of that time and place, Mr. Simmons had missed out on what is usually meant by education, and yet his simple country life had taught him a great deal about people and the world in general. He had lived through hard times and good times, had seen people ruined by both and lifted up by both. He himself had retained a happy, energetic outlook on life, and he had a way of rubbing this off on others. The bright eyes under his receding gray hairline, and his strong, low-pitched voice always gave people the impression that here was a man who faced life without fear, a man with drive and initiative. And yet he was never too proud to ask for advice from anyone, as he did now.

"Where you think Don might have holed up when he got caught by the storm? We're not far from Ogdeen's place. You think he might have stopped in there?"

"Not a chance," said Pete. He leaned forward and tried to press some of the water out of his healthy growth of light-brown hair. "He knows too much about Mr. Ogdeen for him to want to go near the place; and anyhow, it's too close to home. If Don made it that far, he'd be silly not to ride the rest of the way home."

"Oh, I dunno. What if the storm caught up to him just as he went by there? He mighta bin more afraid of the storm than of Ogdeen."

"I doubt it," said Pete. "Anyhow, there's no way we can drive onto Ogdeen's place. It'll be a mess."

"Guess so," agreed his dad. "We don't really have no choice but to stay on this high road. All we can do is keep goin' an' hope we'll meet Don somewhere, but we can turn in an' check at every farm where the lane ain't too bad."

Pete's handsome, strong-featured face looked thoughtful. His mind was still on Mr. Ogdeen. "Dad, Anthony Ogdeen is really a weirdo. I often wonder what's with him anyhow. For a while I thought he might be hiding from the law, but then I remembered how he cussed out some of the people in town. And anyone in hiding wouldn't raise a ruckus like that; he wouldn't want to draw attention to himself."

"Yeah, I doubt he's runnin' from the law," agreed Mr. Simmons. "Might be though. But I got him figured strictly as a mental case. You can see it in his eyes."

"You think he was born that way? Like mentally retarded?"

"No, more 'n likely he thought himself into it. I seen more 'n one good smart man crack up in my time. An' they weren't always in any kind of big trouble. But they got thinkin' in wrong ways—always thinkin' about one thing. It chews on 'em. It keeps chewin' on 'em till it's got a hole chewed in their heads. An' they never think of askin' God for help. If they'd do that they'd soon be all right."

"What do you think could be chewing on Ogdeen?" asked Pete.

"Who knows? But one thing's sure. He's got a mean streak in him twice as wide as this road. He needs help. But how do you help someone if you can't get close to him or can't talk to him?"

"I don't know," said Pete. "Maybe someone should commit him to a mental institution."

"No, that wouldn't be very neighborly. An' we don't really know it would be the best way to help him."

They drove on in silence for a ways, slowly, cautiously, through a dim ocean of pounding water and splashing mud. Some of the gravel had already been washed off the road, but there were old, grooved-in tracks along the center, and so far the truck's wheels tended to follow these shallow ruts rather than skid sideways. As the darkness increased, the flashes of lightning became more spectacular. Mr. Simmons had already switched on the headlights.

They were nearing Ogdeen's lane when they saw Don standing in the middle of the road in front of them. He looked like a drowned-out gopher.

They pulled up to him and got him into the cab. He was shivering and his teeth sounded like loose tappets in a fast-running motor. While Mr. Simmons drove toward the nearest crossroads where he'd be able to turn around, Don gave them a rough outline of what had happened.

He concluded, "After I'd been lying on the creek bank for a while and had some strength back, I started walking. I got into heavy mud in a few places, but I knew if I'd keep going I'd have to hit this road. It wasn't very far. I haven't seen Pedro since I lost him in the creek."

"He might be all right," said Mr. Simmons. "A horse is pretty hard to drown. Anyhow, the main thing is that you're OK."

Mr. Simmons drove slowly and carefully. Several times the pickup began to skid toward the ditch, but always, at the last moment, it would straighten out again.

They finally got to their lane, which by now was so soggy it was almost impassable, and they just barely made it through. As the truck swung into the yard its headlights momentarily lit up the front of the barn. Pedro was standing there, his back hunched, his head hanging down. He had been strong enough to fight his way out of the creek and probably had found a gate leading to the road or else had jumped the fence.

They pulled up close to the jaded animal; Pete climbed out and led Pedro into the barn while the other two went on toward the house. Mr. Simmons brought Don into the brightly lit, warm kitchen where Mrs. Simmons and Julie had been waiting anxiously; then he drove back to the barn to pick up Pete.

And so that evening of trouble finally came to an

end. Mrs. Simmons, a petite, soft-voiced woman who radiated kindness continuously, fixed Don a bathtub full of hot water and told him to soak in it for at least an hour. When he went to bed right after the soaking, he had no trouble falling asleep; and he slept well for most of the night. But toward morning he had a brief nightmare about Anthony Ogdeen with a dagger in one hand and a hangman's noose in the other.

The days that followed were bright and warm. Don's muscles felt so sore for about three days that he didn't do much, but after that he was ready to pitch into the farm work as he had before. Mr. Simmons and Pete both told him that he should just take it easy for a day or two more, but Don insisted and they finally gave in.

This was the middle of the haying season, but because of the big rain the baling had to postponed until the cut hay—which was on slightly lower ground —had dried out. However, on a farm there's always something to do, and Arthur Simmons decided to build a new stretch of fence in the east pasture.

Pete and Don hooked a flat rack (a wagon carrying a wide platform instead of a box) behind the chore tractor and then loaded posts, rolls of wire, staples, and fencing tools onto the rack. They drove out toward the east pasture.

Saskatchewan was beautiful on this bright morning. The land was fairly level here, but it was not open prairie. In the fields and bordering the roadsides were many groves of poplar trees which were bright emerald green and filled with birds' songs. Don sat on the flat rack while Pete guided the small tractor along the gravel road and then down a trail through one of the hayfields. The hay, which had already been cut into swaths, looked in bad shape—beaten down by the rain—but it gave off an aromatic smell as the sun continued to dry it out.

For a few minutes Don got into a daydreamy mood. It was strange and pleasant to be here in another country almost a thousand miles from home. He thought about his friends at his high school, and about the past four years.

Two years ago someone had hung a dumb nickname on him—*Fish*, because he spent so much time in the pool. It had really bothered him. Why couldn't it have been *Speed*, or *Champ* (he had won almost every swimming contest he had ever entered)—but *Fish!*

His senior year had been better than the preceding three. The Christian movement among the kids had gained momentum; there had been more goodwill, understanding, and cooperation, especially among the juniors and seniors, where most of the converts were.

It hadn't all been perfect though. Don had not been afraid to tell others about Jesus, and this in itself had given him some problems, which was to be expected. What really bothered him was that when he shared the Gospel with non-Christians, they very often thought he was not being sincere. And even one

Christian friend had told him: "Don, sometimes I wonder what you're trying to do. You tell people about God's love, but while you're doing it you look about as gentle and loving as a lion-tamer."

How could people say and think things like that? Don was sure he loved others. He was concerned about their welfare. Didn't it show? Did he have to take a course in acting or public speaking or nonverbal communication before he could properly witness for Christ? It didn't seem right.

There *had* been courses available along those lines. The closest thing to it that he had ever taken was a course called "Modern Trends in Philosophy and Psychology," which in part dealt with human communication. And lately he had been reading a lot of books on psychiatry. But apparently it hadn't done much for him.

Don wondered what college would be like—if he went. He still didn't know what he'd do next and this bothered him. But he knew it had to be something that would fit in with his overall plan to spend his life working full time for Christ's cause. In Don's imaginative glimpses into the future he saw himself traveling throughout the whole world and doing something—it wasn't always entirely clear what—to help people out of all kinds of suffering into a happier way of life.

As Don rode the flat rack through Saskatchewan hayfields, his mind took little side trips to Africa, South America, Asia, Europe, and back to his own continent. In each place he visualized ugly things that needed changing. In Africa, for instance, he saw backwoods tribesmen hiring a witch doctor to put the death hex on an enemy, a hex that would work, for the witch doctor would see to it in one way or another that the victim died.

If Pete, on the tractor up ahead, had suddenly been able to see all the colorful and dreadful population riding along on the flat rack with Don, it might have frightened him half to death.

Although Don often let his mind wander to faraway places and get involved in imaginative events, this morning he had been doing so, and also thinking about the other things, mainly to keep from dwelling on his experience in the flood and with Ogdeen four days ago. But, as usual, he was successful in this only for a while. The round, angry, unhappy face of Ogdeen kept floating back into his consciousness no matter how often Don banished it, and so did the roar of white-foaming floodwater. It was definitely unpleasant.

Leaving the hayfield, Pete and Don crossed over a road, then passed through an open gate into the pasture. Pete swung right and immediately came to a stop beside the strip of ramshackle fence that ran parallel with the road.

Don and Pete walked a short distance alongside the fence, checking to see how bad it was, and then came back to the wagon.

"You've been kind of quiet so far today," noted Pete

as he hoisted three of the new posts onto his broad shoulder. "Are you still brooding about Ogdeen?"

"Yeah, some," said Don. "Pete, that man is danger-ous. If I hadn't left when I did, there's no telling what might have happened. You should have seen the hatred in his eyes!"

Pete walked three steps over to the ragged fence and dropped off one of the new posts. As usual, he appeared to be bursting with energy. His expressive, handsome face almost always carried a look of con-tentment, and he smiled often. He seemed to stay happy through rain, shine, and mosquitoes.

"You could be right," he said as he walked over to the next bad post. "Dad and I have talked about it quite a bit lately. Dad now thinks it might be a good idea to let the police know about him. We'd probably be doing Mr. Ogdeen a favor to get him to somebody who could give him the right kind of help—psychiatric help."

"That's right," agreed Don, "and that might pre-vent him from being a danger to others."

Don began to pull staples out of the old fence posts where the wire was not already hanging loose. The two boys worked their way along the bad stretch, now and then moving the tractor and flat rack. In about an hour they had all the new posts laid out and had the old barbed wire pulled down. The wire would have to be rolled up by hand, a prickly, springy, uncomforta-ble job, and human nature dictated that they put this off until later. So they simply pulled the loose strands far enough to one side so they'd have room to dig new holes. They did the digging with a portable post-hole auger that they connected to the power take-off shaft at the rear of the tractor. Although the fence line was on comparatively high ground, the soil was still extra soft from the big rain four days ago, and so the digging was easy.

Don drove the tractor, stopping at the right places along the fence line, and Pete controlled the auger. As it spun rapidly under his hands he would let it sink smoothly into the moist earth a good three feet, almost the full length of the digging shaft. Then he'd quickly pull it back out, and Don, watching carefully from the tractor, would put his foot on the clutch to disengage the power take-off so that the auger would stop spinning. Then they'd move on to the next place, Pete carrying the heavy auger.

They were still working at this, taking turns on the auger, when the half-ton pickup pulled up and Mr. Simmons stepped out on the driver's side. On the other side Julie climbed out holding a dinner basket. She was wearing a cute green dress that looked a touch too fine for a workday on the farm. The pleasant thought passed through Don's mind that maybe she had prettied up like that today especially for him. But it seemed more likely that she was ready to go somewhere, maybe to the nearby city of Saskatoon for shopping. Don shut off the tractor and got down.

Pete said, "Didn't know it was anywhere near noon. I must have been enjoying my work."

"It's twelve-thirty," said Julie as she set the basket on the pickup's tailgate which Mr. Simmons had lowered into a horizontal position so it could be used as a table.

"Well, I'm hungry enough," said Pete.

"What about you, Don?" asked Julie.

"Oh, I'm hungry," he replied. Every time Julie spoke to him he got funny feelings all through his bones. She had a pleasant, energetic, friendly way about her, and she was so pretty. Her only blemish, if it could be called that, was the round birthmark about the size of a nailhead on her left cheek. Whenever she smiled, the brown mark partly disappeared in a dimple. Just as her brother had the light-brown hair and big frame of his father, so Julie had inherited the luxuriant dark hair and small, lithe figure of her mother. Julie looked almost too delicate to be very athletic, but Don had seen her riding galloping horses and sometimes handling heavy hay bales. Farm girls, Don was beginning to realize, were strange, interesting, and paradoxical creatures.

As the four people settled on and around the truck box it was inevitable that their conversation should center on Anthony Ogdeen.

Julie sat on the tailgate beside the dinner basket. She gave Don an unpleasant surprise when she said, "If you want my honest opinion, I think everyone should just leave him alone. Why go tell him that Christianity has all the answers to his problems? Maybe he doesn't want any answers to his problems.

Maybe he likes problems." She shrugged her small shoulders a couple of times in a gesture that was somewhat habitual with her.

Mr. Simmons sat in the truck box on the rounded metal edge, leaning forward so that his chin seemed to be resting on the baggy bib of his overalls. He wasn't wearing a cap, and the breeze had blown a thin wisp of gray hair down over his serious face.

"Now, Julie, you know he's an unhappy man. He's lonely and he's full of hate. He needs someone to come along an' tell him about God's love. Don did the right thing when he went in there an' tried to talk to him."

"I don't see it," said Julie, keeping her eyes to the ground.

Don was so shocked by her words he stopped chewing. He probably would have asked her to explain her attitude, but just then they heard the sound of a rapidly approaching vehicle. In a few moments a blue hardtop pulled to a stop on the road bordering the fence line.

It was Anthony Ogdeen. He got out and stood beside his car. Today he was dressed in colorful outdoor clothing, including an English-style hunting cap.

"Don Shield," he called, "would you come over here a moment? I'd like to talk to you."

Don walked over to the bulky man. In the car's back seat were camping equipment and a folding artist's easel. Apparently Ogdeen was starting out on a trip of some kind.

The artist spoke to Don in a low voice so that the others wouldn't hear. "I just wanted to tell you," said the round, intense face, "that you're not welcome at my place anymore. We have nothing in common, nothing to talk about. You provoked me to the point where I lost control of myself, and that's something I can do without. So from now on stay away from me with your Christianity!" Ogdeen turned his back on Don and climbed into the car. A moment later there was spraying mud and then the quickly diminishing sound of a powerful V-8 motor.

Don took the whole thing quite personally. Although he would have hated to admit it, he was really much less concerned about the rebuff given to Christianity than about the snub he himself had received. As he walked back toward the others he was so full of frustration and anger that he thought he might pop like an overstretched balloon. The ugly feelings showed plainly in his face.

Pete was leaning against the truck box. He said, "Don, remember what it says in the Bible: 'Love your enemies, do good to those who hate you, bless those who curse you, and pray for those who mistreat you.'"

But Don's mood was so black that he barely heard the words of his friend.

8

Ogdeen's Trip

The artist from Los Angeles drove his car northward through the beautiful Saskatchewan summer
afternoon.

Ogdeen, in spite of his overweight, could have
looked fairly handsome that day. He was dressed in
outdoor clothing that suited his massive build, and
the Sherlock Holmes type of hunting cap fighting to
hold down his shaggy hair went well with the rugged,
heavy features of his face.

But the expression on that face was ugly enough to
completely cancel out the pleasing aspects of his appearance. It was an expression of smoldering hatred
and anger. He was in a very bad mood. For some
reason he had been in that mood ever since he got up
in the morning, and his second encounter with the
kid just now hadn't helped.

Ogdeen knew that his emotions were unstable, but
he had learned to accept this as something to be lived
with. Until a few years ago he had refused to admit to

himself that there was anything wrong, but his angry outbursts and other demonstrations of hostility had finally resulted in his being committed, quite against his will, to a mental institution in Los Angeles. He had been kept there for seven months and during that time had found more peace and tranquillity than he had ever known in any other situation.

Even now he could sometimes calm an angry mood to some extent by thinking about that place—its pleasant grounds with walks winding through flowers and trees, the group discussions where he could express himself on his deepest concerns to surprisingly attentive ears, and best of all the psychiatrists who took such a sincere, personal interest in him.

They were intelligent, thinking men; they were not fools. They understood something about how the human mind works. And they had helped him. For one thing, they got him to admit to himself that there *was* something wrong. They had told him he was emotionally unstable and that he had psychopathic antisocial tendencies.

Once he had accepted this, Ogdeen had never really changed his mind on it; and by now he had learned to live with his violent moods in such a way that he usually managed to stay out of trouble, at least the more serious kinds of trouble.

He believed that he was being very patient with his fellowmen in so controlling himself; for although he accepted the fact that he had an emotion-control problem, he was even more convinced that the world in general deserved the unleashing of his righteous wrath. He had plans. Someday he would stop holding back. But not yet.

Rather than tangle with people all the time, as he used to do before his stay at the institution, he now tried to avoid them as much as possible. It was because of this rule that he had decided it was best to tell the kid not to come back for another visit.

But the encounter at the pasture fence had upset Ogdeen more than he had expected. The kid hadn't said a word; he had just looked at him with those big soft eyes like a dumb animal about to be slaughtered. He should have cussed, or at least turned his back and walked away. Instead he had stood there like a—like a fool, decided Ogdeen vehemently. His mood had been softening a little, but now it grew worse.

Fools! Fools! Fools! thought Ogdeen. *How can they ever learn? The utter stupidity of it all! Rebuilding barbed-wire fences that should have been obsolete centuries ago, and would have been, along with a lot of other stupid things, if it weren't for the many people who are just like those miserable fools I left at the roadside. Christians! They're the worst kind! Do they think they're being useful? What are they doing? Building stupid fences to keep their stupid cows out of their stupid fields or inside of them—what's the difference? If it wasn't for Christians having held back technological progress for the last 2,000 years, there would no longer be any need for cows, fields, and fences. There'd be plenty of synthetic food for* everyone. And best of all, people would be using their minds and talking intelligently instead of coming around and telling me I need to have my soul saved!

At this last thought Ogdeen became so incensed that he tried to choke his steering wheel to death. After a few seconds of this his anger subsided somewhat, and then it slowly changed into a self-pity type of sadness.

Maybe I should have stayed in Los Angeles. At least I was in contact with a few intelligent persons there. Even after I got out of the institution. That was a nice meeting place we had on Wilshire Boulevard. For a while I thought we were going to make real progress. But they were all too scared. I kept telling them over and over that the only way technology and science would ever win out over the mysticism of Christians would be by force—violent force. They agreed with my thinking—they agreed, of course, that any suffering that came upon the fools didn't matter—but they were scared. They kept saying we were too few in number, and I kept telling them that a start had to be made sometime if anything was ever going to be done.

I couldn't stand the delay anymore so I really had to get away from them too. I had to get away to think and to plan and to raise money with my paintings, for money will be needed to buy guns and ammunition. It won't be long before I have enough new paintings done so that I can open another art show in L.A. But in the meantime how can I think or plan or paint when my own house is invaded by a soul-saving Christian?

Then Ogdeen's mouth curved into a cruel smile. *That young fool! Ha! There's only one thing to do with him!*

After that, Ogdeen became more tranquil, and instead of staring straight ahead at the road he began to glance from side to side as though enjoying the scenery.

A quarter of a mile later he suddenly let the speed of his car fall sharply. On his left was a closed gate leading into a pasture. Ogdeen turned toward it and pulled to a stop. He got out, opened the gate, and drove through. Then he stood beside his car and looked straight ahead.

"Beautiful!" he exclaimed, and he was right. Lush pastureland was framed by several huge old maple trees growing nearby on either side of the car. Here and there in the distance were bright-colored patches of weed flowers. Still farther away the meadow came to an end against a dark green curtain of towering pine trees, the outer sentinels of a vast provincial forest reserve. Above the pines lay a gold tinged haze of cloud, and higher up the sky was a deep, clean, translucent blue.

Ogdeen turned to his car and yanked open a rear door. With great haste he began to unload his art equipment. He knew from past experience how quickly a scene can be altered because of changing light; those misty, golden clouds just above the horizon would probably not be there for more than a couple of minutes.

In a few seconds he had set up his easel, slapped a twenty-four-by-eighteen-inch stretched canvas onto it, and opened a fresh box of pastel-colored chalk. This chalk was only for the preliminary sketching, in place of charcoal. He liked using color for the sketch because that way he could quickly capture some of the more temporary hues of cloud and sky.

Standing in front of his tall easel, Ogdeen rapidly began to draw a rough outline of the distant pine trees. Then, with this horizon line as a guide, he lost no time in attempting to represent the beautiful misty clouds that floated just above. When he had finished that part of the sketch to his satisfaction, he put in graceful outlines of the maple trees that grew nearby on either side; and finally, with a few quick sweeps of variously colored chalk, he suggested the hues of grass and weeds on the pasture floor.

Now Ogdeen adjusted the canvas so it hung lower on the easel; then he brought a folding stool from the car. He sat down in front of his work so he'd be comfortable and steady for the more detailed part of his sketch that was to follow. Although he still used only chalk and occasionally a soft lead pencil, this latest portion of the work took him the best part of an hour.

Now the preliminary sketch was complete. Ogdeen sat back and studied it with satisfaction. The misty, yellow clouds were beautiful; the expanse of unruffled pasture held a feeling of peacefulness and pleasant summer warmth; the maple trees arched their long branches gracefully across the top of the picture, and—from one of the branches dangled the form of a dying youth, his neck in a hangman's noose. Although the victim's face was distorted by agony, the clean-lined features were easily recognizable. It was the face of Don Shield.

Ogdeen told himself he had done enough work for the day. The sketch was finished; tomorrow he would begin to paint it, probably in acrylics rather than oil because oil dries so slowly. It was time now to start thinking about setting up camp and cooking supper.

Within an hour Ogdeen had pitched a tent, unrolled his sleeping bag, and set up a camp stove. Soon he had beans and coffee bubbling over the gas flame.

Doing the sketch had released some of Ogdeen's anger, but not all of it. As he started to eat he was still thinking about Don's visit during the storm. Now the artist tried to banish the matter from his mind, but it kept coming back.

Blast it! he told himself. *I thought just about all the Gospel-preaching Christians in the world were bunched up in Los Angeles. It sure seemed that way; they kept popping up all the time. I thought once I'd get out of L.A. I'd have left them behind. So I buy an old secluded farmstead in Canada and keep out of everybody's way, and what happens? Ha! As if the village pastor isn't bad enough! In marches a long-legged kid and tells me—tells me—he tells me that I won't be happy and have peace until I get right with*

*God, and that the way to get right with God is through
Jesus Christ.*

Ogdeen poured himself a cup of coffee and wondered why he was letting his mind dwell on the kid's
words. He would stop that right now. *He said he felt
sorry for me!*

Abruptly, in a gesture of fury directed mainly at his
own inability to control his thoughts, Ogdeen threw
his full cup out through the open doorway of the tent.

He ate a bit, then crawled outside to retrieve his
cup. After finishing the beans and half a pot of black
coffee, Ogdeen just sat and continued to brood. As
usual after a bout of uncontrolled anger, he now experienced a mixed-up feeling of depression that was
largely guilt; but he was not about to admit to himself
that he actually felt guilty. Sometimes he did so, but
tonight his ego was still too big and bold for that.

Ogdeen spent a comfortable night in his tent. He
arose just before sunrise, and after another half a pot
of coffee he once more set up his easel. This time he
got out a box of acrylic paints, some brushes, and
water for mixing. Soon he was hard at work rendering
his sketch in glistening, moist colors. He continued to
paint all morning, seldom stopping for a break, and
by noon he had finished the sky and had a good start
on the figure of the youth.

Just as Ogdeen was about to lay down his brush and
stop for dinner, he was surprised by the appearance of
four cows, huge red and white creatures with long
horns. No doubt he would have noticed their ap-

proach sooner if he hadn't been so absorbed in his work.

The cows didn't pay much attention to him, but all at once they broke into a run and dashed between his easel and the car, charging out through the gate that Ogdeen hadn't bothered to close.

Now a harsh-sounding voice yelled, "Hey! What's the big idea?"

Ogdeen glanced up and saw an angry-faced little man running toward him. He was obviously a farmer, for he wore a beat-up straw hat and coveralls liberally decorated with grease and manure.

"Why'd you leave the gate open?" he asked as he came to a stop before the artist who was still sitting in front of his painting. "And how come you're camping here in the first place? At least you could have closed the gate! Now my cows got out. Well, you'll just have to help me bring 'em back in."

"Forget it," said Ogdeen, not bothering to even look at the farmer. "I'm not about to start chasing after some stupid cows."

For a moment the farmer was speechless, then he said, "Well, you've got your nerve! You come in here and camp on my land without asking permission, set up a camp and litter up the place, leave my gate open so my cows run away, and then when I ask you to help me bring 'em back in, you give me that kind of answer! Well, let me tell you something! I don't have your name, but I have your car plate number and you're in trouble!" He began to walk past Ogdeen toward the gate.

Ogdeen sprang to his feet. The little farmer, thinking this might be a physical attack, quickly spun around to face him.

Now the two men stood glaring at each other. Ogdeen had turned white with rage. "Let me tell you something!" he exploded. "If you aren't out of my sight within thirty seconds I'll break your scrawny neck!" He added a long streak of solid cursing, then finished with: "Go to the police if you like! You think a fine would bother me? Do you think the threat of that could scare me into taking orders from a crummy two-bit hayseed with manure on his pants? Your thirty seconds are running out—fast!"

The little farmer valued his life and health enough so that he turned and walked off. He went back the way he had come, no longer bothering about his cows. But once he had put a safer distance between himself and the maniac, he called over his shoulder: "You just wait right there where you are. I have three six-footer sons I'd like you to meet!"

"Bring whoever you like!" yelled Ogdeen. "I'll mangle you all in a bunch or one at a time, whichever you prefer!" He doubted that the farmer really had any "six-footer" sons, yet he realized that this had to be considered as a serious possibility. Although he was in an almost mindless rage, Ogdeen's strong instinct of self-preservation wouldn't allow him to wait around for three or four men to come and beat him up.

But the artist gave himself a full minute for throwing things around, including his tent, his camp stove, and some cans of pork and beans. Then he collected it all together from where he had scattered it and flung it pell-mell into the back seat of the car. However, he was more careful with his art equipment; with the half-finished painting he actually controlled himself long enough to lock it away safely in the trunk.

That done, he shouted a few curses after the farmer—who had long been out of sight and was probably out of earshot as well—before he climbed behind the wheel of his car. The motor roared to life and the vehicle jumped forward into a sharp turn. Wheels spinning on the grass, Ogdeen headed toward the gate. He thought of running down one of the corner posts, but again self-preservation made him choose a wiser course. Without actually thinking about it, he realized that the way things stood right now there was a good chance that the farmer wouldn't go to the police; he might be satisfied to think he had frightened Ogdeen away by telling him he was going to return with his sons. But if he came back and found a broken gate he would surely go to the law and file a complaint.

So Ogdeen cleared the corner post and skidded his car onto the road, heading in the same direction he had been traveling the previous day. He floored the gas pedal. The big V-8 motor grabbed the wheels and spun mud twleve feet into the air. The car shot northward farther along the road that led toward the forest reserve.

Ogdeen drove and cursed and thought. He thought about what he'd like to do to that little farmer. By the time he had narrowed the matter down to half a dozen gruesome choices, he was already deciding on what size the picture would be and that he would do it in heavy oils with no mixer added.

Ogdeen was so enshrouded by his angry, sadistic thoughts that he didn't really notice the rapidly passing scenery changing from lush grass and poplar bush to a more rugged type of vegetation. The grass turned scraggly; the poplars were replaced by crooked jack pines. The muddy road became a sandy trail as rich farm soil gave way to the less productive forest-reserve area.

Now the trail curved smoothly through a growth of pines and then climbed a low hill where there were no trees. As he sped over the crest, Ogdeen's heavy-featured face broke into an evil smile, for he had just decided definitely that in his next painting he would have the little farmer clubbed to death by another man. And that other man in the picture would be Anthony Ogdeen.

Suddenly the car lurched sideways violently as the two right-side wheels hit a ridge of loose sand. The skidding vehicle left the road entirely and a short second later it was leaping off the hillside. As the falling car tilted nose downward, Ogdeen saw that he was plunging into a deep gully.

Ogdeen's emotions did a very quick change from flaming anger to soul-freezing fear of death.

9

Emergency

The hay was almost dry; it would soon be ready for baling. At ten o'clock in the morning, two days after Don and the others had last seen Ogdeen, Mr. Simmons and Pete went out to check the hayfields.

In the meantime Don helped Julie with the halter-breaking of her 4-H calf in preparation for the achievement day to be held in less than a week's time. On that day all the local members of the 4-H Club would bring their special animals, well fattened and groomed, to a competitive beef show. There would be a large assortment of ribbons, banners, trophies, and cash awards to be won, for the contest categories ranged from beef conformation to showmanship with several lesser competitions in between.

"How can you call this a calf?" Don asked Julie. "It's too big to be called a calf." The yearling Charolais-cross steer weighed at least a thousand pounds, and his back was on a level with Don's chest.

"Maybe you're right," replied Julie. Even in her chore clothes—faded jeans and blue cotton blouse —she was neat and tidy. And it seemed that her long dark hair always looked just right around her pretty face, no matter from which direction the wind happened to be blowing.

Julie led the yellow-orange beast toward the flat rack and tractor with the intention of tying him to the rack so that she could then start the tractor and lead him about the yard in this way. He was already fairly well halter-broke, but occasionally turned stubborn. Julie hoped that leading him behind the tractor and wagon would cure him. But now, before she could get him there, the big yellow steer decided he had gone far enough for the time being. Julie's tugging and coaxing made no difference.

Don saw this as an opportunity to go to the rescue. He approached the girl and her jumbo pet with a wonderful feeling of manliness. "Here," he said, reaching for the halter shank, "let me try."

"Oh, thanks," said Julie.

"What's his name? He might come better if I call his name."

"Anchor."

"Huh?"

"His name is Anchor," said Julie. "As you can guess, this isn't the first time he has refused to move."

"Hm, well, I'll make him come. C'mon, Anchor, c'mon, boy!" Don began to pull on the lead, gently at first, then harder and harder.

Julie looked a little guilty. "I guess there's some-thing I should tell you—two things, in fact."

Don had become very determined. "Tell me later. Right now this—this—'calf' is going to move! C'mon, boy, come on!"

Suddenly the lead rope parted from the halter, and Don fell on his back with his legs high in the air. As he scrambled to his feet he expected Anchor to run away, but the beast just stood there looking at him, as if he were laughing silently. There was no doubt about Julie's laughter.

She finally got her merriment under control enough so that she could speak. "One of the things I was going to tell you is that the snap fastener on the rope doesn't work so good. If you pull too hard it comes undone."

Don picked up his hat while he brushed dust from his jeans. "And what's the other thing you were going to tell me?" he asked glumly.

Julie was already fixing the rope back onto the halter. "Well, I was just going to tell you that when Anchor doesn't want to come, I have a cool secret weapon for making him move." She reached into the pocket of her blouse and took out a sugar lump. "This is the secret weapon. Come, Anchor. Would you like some sugar?" She held the bait just far enough from the steer's nose so that in order to reach it he would have to take a step forward. He did so. But Julie drew the lure back and soon had the big animal eagerly following along behind her. She tied him to the wagon and then rewarded him with two sugar lumps.

"You're not mad at me, are you?" Julie asked Don. "I mean for the way I laughed at you." And she laughed some more.

"No, I'm not," said Don. His good humor actually was returning quite nicely. He laughed now too. "I guess it was a reasonably good joke on me."

Suddenly Julie's pretty face turned serious. "That's what I like about you Christians," she said with a touch of irony in her voice. "You're always so cheerful."

This statement hit Don like a shotgun blast. Even though he had heard Julie say disturbing things about Christianity, he had kept hoping she was a believer. Now she had shattered that hope by saying "you Christians."

Julie noticed the look on his face. "Don't take another header," she said as she sat down on the flat rack close to her calf. "I've just decided to stop being a hypocrite. It's probably very sinful to be a hypocrite. Don't you think so?"

Don took a few unconscious steps toward her. He said, "Julie, I thought all along you were a Christian, like Pete and your mom and dad. In fact, that's what Pete told me when we first met in Minneapolis."

"Don't blame Pete. He thought he was telling the truth."

"You mean you lied to him and to your mom and dad about it?"

"Well, maybe not outright. I used to kind of hedge around and give them the impression that I was a Christian. And I went to church so willingly and regularly that I guess I had them fooled. But I'm disgusted with myself for playing that kind of game. I won't do it anymore."

Don sat down on the flat rack a few feet away from the dark-haired girl. Her large, brown, serious eyes met his unwaveringly when he spoke.

"What's your way of thinking about it then, Julie? Are you against Christianity, or are you trying to find out the truth about it?"

"I want to know the truth," she said, her eyelids dropping. Maybe she wasn't entirely sure that her answer was honest. She seemed to be battling with the matter. "Yes, I really want to know the truth about it. And, in a way I hope I find out that Christianity is true. If it's like it says in the Bible, then Jesus is the most wonderful Person who ever lived."

"He's the most wonderful Person *living*," corrected Don. "And He suffered and died on the cross, and rose again to life in order to give you a new life."

"New life," echoed Julie. "That's exactly where I start running into trouble about the whole thing."

"What do you mean?"

"Christians are always talking about the new life they have 'in Christ Jesus.'" She shrugged her shoulders and tossed her hair back. "But why should I think that Christians are really anything different?"

"Well, *my* life changed when I let Jesus take over. I

didn't become perfect, but I *did* get a new way of thinking about everything. I want to do what God wants me to do. And now I'm trying to let that new nature have control over the rest of me."

"That's what Christians say, isn't it? But if the new nature you're talking about *doesn't* have control—if it doesn't really change a person's way of living—then how can anyone prove that he's got anything from God?"

"Well, it *does* change a person's life. Haven't you noticed it in Pete and your parents and in probably a lot of other Christians you know?"

"Oh, I don't know." Her shoulders jumped up again. "They're mostly all pretty human, really. Take Pete, for instance. He's what you might call an all-the-way Christian. I mean he's—y'know, saved. But is there anything really different about him? Does he plan on sacrificing his whole life to the cause? He has plans for his life like anyone else. I can remember that ever since we were little kids he's had his heart set on becoming a doctor, so—"

"A doctor! Pete?"

"Right. That's what he still wants. He's never told you, eh?"

"No, I mean, it seems so strange. Pete is the outdoor type all the way. It seems silly to think of him as a doctor."

"I know," agreed Julie. Anchor was pulling on his rope, so Julie got out another lump of sugar. "But that's what he wants. And knowing Pete, I'd say nothing is going to stop him."

"Yeah," said Don. "But anyhow, what's wrong with being a doctor? He can do a lot of good as a doctor."

"That's not the point," replied Julie. Anchor was slobbering all over her hand, but that didn't bother Julie, a farm girl who was used to feeding sugar lumps to cattle and horses. She wiped her hand on the steer's neck. "It's his motive I'm thinking of."

"Well, what do you think it is?" asked Don, almost afraid to ask.

"He wants to get filthy rich," stated Julie.

"Aw no," said Don, shaking his head slowly. "I know doctors latch onto a lot of bread, but I'm sure Pete will have a better motive than that." He rubbed his chin as he thought more about it. Then he remembered something Pete had said a few days earlier. "Pete mentioned to me not long ago that he thinks one of the greatest things holding back the spread of the Gospel is that Christians aren't willing enough to financially support evangelistic and missionary work. If Pete should ever make a lot of money, I really think he'd use it for the cause of Christ to help people out of suffering and to help spread the Gospel. I haven't known Pete for very long, but I don't doubt his honesty. In no way is he a hypocrite. And I think, Julie, that if you were honest with yourself you'd know it too."

Julie slipped down off the rack. *Maybe she is going*

to end the conversation and go on with her work, Don thought. But she said, "I suppose I'm just a doubting Thomas, but I always have my doubts about people's motives for the things they do, including Christians."

When Julie didn't turn away, Don asked, "What are your own plans and dreams for the future? I mean in the line of work."

Julie leaned her slim figure against the flat rack and gazed off into space. Suddenly she laughed and said with a put-on air of happy fervor, "I want to be free!" And she flung out her arms in a dramatic gesture. Then she sat down on the rack again, now on the other side of Don. She said, "I want to travel, travel, travel—over the whole world."

"Great," said Don, "but that isn't work."

"I know, but that's what I'd like to do—to be completely free to go where I want, when I want."

"All by yourself?"

"No, I'd like to be with somebody."

"A man, maybe?"

Julie looked at him and smiled so that the birthmark half disappeared in the dimple. "Sure, why not? I'd like to get married someday to a man who also wants to be free and to travel all over the world."

Don was amused and pleased by her adventurous spirit, and his heart went out to her more than ever before. Wasn't this the kind of girl he had often dreamed about, one who shared his own liking for adventure and travel? But as he thought about the matter he began to see more clearly into the girl's heart.

"Julie," he said, "is that why you're refusing Christ? Do you think He'd take away your freedom or your chances for freedom?"

The birthmark popped back to its normal place and Julie's eyes widened ever so slightly. Don knew he had hit a nerve. Even though he had been fairly successful in making a habit of daily Bible reading, he was no good at quoting Scripture; so he paraphrased the verse he was thinking of.

"What good will it do you, Julie, if you get the whole world to travel around in, but lose your own soul?" She didn't answer but just kept looking at him, so he continued.

"There's nothing wrong with traveling, and there's nothing wrong with wanting to be free in the right way—free under God. God wants us to have a lot of freedom, but He knows that we need Him as our Father to guide us and take care of us."

Julie looked down and raised up the pointed toe of one riding boot a little, as though to study it better. "I know Christians have to put God first, above all else, and that's as it should be. I don't know. It's just that I don't trust people's sincerity. God's children don't always behave like God's children, and that makes me wonder, makes me doubt Christianity too much to just accept it just like that."

"No one becomes perfect in a flash when they're saved," said Don. "It's called the new birth; after the birth comes the growing and changing." Don suddenly realized that in all the Christian witnessing he had ever done, he had never felt the way he did right now. It had always been a matter of just stating the facts and leaving it at that, but now his whole being seemed to be reaching out toward Julie.

The girl lowered herself from the flat rack again and stood so that her face was partly turned away from Don. She said, "Maybe if I could find one Christian—just one—who behaved like a Christian *all* the time, maybe then I could accept what you're telling me. Maybe then I'd know that Christianity is more than talking."

Before Don could reply, Pete's dog, Collie, began to bark loudly as he ran across the yard toward the long, tree-bordered lane.

"What a dumb dog!" said Julie. "He still doesn't recognize our own truck. Pete must be driving; Dad drives slower."

"I'd say that's a little too fast even for Pete," observed Don. "I hope nothing's wrong."

By the time the half-ton pickup pulled up at the big two-story house, Julie and Don were halfway across the yard. Mr. Simmons got out and hurried toward the house, while Pete jumped out from the driver's side and with long steps strode to meet them. He stopped in front of Don.

"How would you like to become a volunteer searcher?" he asked.

"Huh?"

"Anthony Ogdeen is missing," explained Pete. "He may be hurt. A couple of Mounties stopped near the hayfield and talked to Dad and me about it. They're looking for information on Ogdeen, and also for volunteers to help search the area where he disappeared. They found his car not far from the Riverside Community Pasture where you rode to check on our cattle the other day, and the car was smashed up at the bottom of a deep gully beside the road. It's a sandy trail, and the police think he must have been driving too fast and lost control in the loose sand. So his car is there, but there's no sign of Ogdeen. They think he might be lost in the community pasture or in the provincial forest reserve right next to it. Anyhow, Dad and I volunteered to go help search. And the police said we should try to round up as many volunteers as we could."

Julie said, "I'll go!"

"You'll come, Don, won't you?" asked Pete.

Don was thinking of the way Anthony Ogdeen had treated him. Although he wanted to help search, he didn't feel quite as enthusiastic about it as he might have under other circumstances. He said, "Well, sure, I'll go."

Julie looked at him. "You don't seem very anxious to help."

Pete told his sister, "That's not a very nice thing to say. And as for you helping, there is something you can do. You can lend me your horse. Don will ride Pedro."

Don was surprised. "We're going on horseback?"

"Yep, the Mounties are asking for horses as well as men. There's a lot of rough country there. But most of the searchers will be on foot. Dad will be going with the truck. I guess he went into the house now to tell Mom about it."

"Then I'll go along with him," said Julie, turning and walking toward the house.

"Come on," Pete said, "let's go saddle up the horses. Ogdeen may be hurt pretty badly. He could even be dying somewhere. The sooner we get started, the better."

10

The Whipping

Ogdeen didn't know how long he had been unconscious. His head hurt and he was cold and wet. Pain
shot through his stiff body as he rolled out of the
shallow puddle of water in which he had been lying.
The sun was shining brightly but he was in the shade
of some tall trees. Songbirds were chirping merrily all
around.

The artist looked as rough as he felt. His shirt and
pants were ripped into rags and almost completely
covered with wet mud. He had lost his cap; his hair
stood out wildly like half a dozen kinky horns. On his
black and blue forehead was a crust of dried blood.

Ogdeen crawled out into the sunshine. The effort
made his head swim, so he stopped and sat on his
heels. He looked all around, wondering where he
was. After a moment he remembered the accident,
how his car had left the road and he had plunged

down toward the bottom of a ravine. But he couldn't remember hitting the bottom or what had happened after that.

He touched his aching forehead and when he took his fingers away they were red. Now he could feel the blood slowly trickling around one eyebrow and down the side of his face. The slight exertion of crawling had been enough to renew the bleeding. Nevertheless, he struggled to his feet and staggered forward, determined to find his car. All his art equipment was in there, and the half-finished painting of Don Shield. He remembered how pleased he was with that piece of work. He mustn't lose it.

He wobbled around from one clearing to another until he came to one that opened into a wide stretch of flat, treeless prairie. So he turned about and went back the other way, but the farther he walked and the more he studied his surroundings, the more he became convinced that he wasn't anywhere near the site of his accident. There the terrain had been rough, with tall pine trees growing out of sandy soil; here the grass-covered ground was level and there were large groves of leafy poplars.

As he walked on, Ogdeen tried hard to remember more of what had happened. He didn't feel very successful in this, but he vaguely recalled having had some sort of a dream while he was unconscious. It was a muddled dream in which he had been first climbing, then walking, stumbling, getting up and walking on again through the darkness—on and on and on. *No,* thought Ogdeen suddenly. *That was no dream! I really was walking!*

No wonder this place looked so different. Half conscious, he had wandered away from his wrecked vehicle and somehow had found his way out of the ravine. Maybe he had walked for hours; it seemed like that. Maybe he was miles from his car.

He stood there shivering in the sunlight. A fire. That's what he needed so he could get warm and dried out. He found a book of paper matches in his pocket and was glad to see that they were dry. Then he went around gathering up twigs, dry leaves, and weeds, and also some larger wood. He took it all to the sunny side of a clearing and built his bonfire.

It felt pretty good with the fire on one side of him and the sun on the other. His head was still bleeding slightly, but it didn't hurt quite so much anymore.

Ogdeen soon felt well enough so that he once again began to think and brood in his normal way. He was still worried about losing the painting he had started yesterday, and this swung his mind back to his hatred of Don Shield and the Christianity the boy stood for. And Ogdeen decided that he just couldn't be satisfied only with painting a picture of what he would like to see done to Don. No, in this case there had to be something more. But what? It had to be something that would directly affect Don. It had to be something that would destroy him in one way or another. Yes, something that would utterly destroy his faith in Christianity and reduce him to a broken, useless

husk. *There must be a way*, thought Ogdeen, *to prove
to him that he's just as selfish and dishonest as anyone else. There must be some way to shake his so-
called faith to its very roots.* As Ogdeen continued to
think about the matter, he got a pencil stub out of his
pocket and doodled on the inside of the matchbook
cover. Doing this helped him to think in a more relaxed way. But, although he doodled for quite some
time, he failed to come up with anything that really
satisfied him.

He didn't give up though, and was still thinking
about the matter when he went to collect more wood
for the fire. There were plenty of dry branches lying
around within the groves of poplar trees. As Ogdeen
walked into the bush he felt his first pang of hunger.
He knew he'd have to start walking and looking for a
road as soon as possible. His hunger wasn't the worst
of it, for his head certainly needed medical attention.
Another night in the open might be too much. But he
did want to dry out completely first, so he was glad
that he'd have a little more time to sit by the fire and
try to think up a way to unleash his hatred on that
blasted kid in blue jeans.

No one but Don Shield had dared to bring his
philosophy of Christianity right into Ogdeen's home.
Well, thought the artist, *when I get through with him
he won't ever again disturb anyone with his faith.* For
a moment Ogdeen had a kind of twisted feeling of
altruism about this, but then he remembered that
according to his own philosophy he wasn't supposed

to care about others. This slip of thought made him all the more furious and more confused; and when he found a thick, dry branch, he immediately used it to strike the nearest tree.

He whipped the tree until the branch in his hands shattered into several pieces and he was left holding a short stick. His head throbbed and a wave of dizziness almost swept him to the ground. He staggered but kept his balance, then started weaving his way back toward the campfire. Before he got clear of the bush, another hard attack of dizziness came upon him, and at that moment his toe hooked on an exposed root. He pitched forward and struck his head against the trunk of a poplar tree.

For a few seconds he lay there twitching, but then he became motionless except for the rising and falling of his chest. The wound on his forehead, now reopened, rapidly spread blood over his relaxed face.

In the clear sky above, a magpie circled lazily and then came and perched on a high branch. He cocked his head sideways so that his beady eye could look down at the motionless form below. Like all magpies, he was always on the lookout for any wounded or dead animal. More of the long-tailed, carnivorous birds soon arrived. They also chose high perches. However, as moments passed and as the prostrate thing on the ground below remained motionless, all of the birds began to move downward among the branches, cautiously but eagerly.

11

The Search

When Lion and Pete pulled their horses to a stop and dismounted at the scene of the accident, the search for Anthony Ogdeen was already well under way.

Sergeant Fisher of the Royal Canadian Mounted Police, the man in charge of the search, met the boys and thanked them for coming. "I'm glad you brought horses," he added. "We'll be able to put them to good use." The young sergeant had on a wide, stiff-brimmed hat; navy breeches with a gold stripe down each side; high, close-fitting riding boots; and a brown thigh-length jacket or tunic. The traditional scarlet jackets were now used only for ceremonial occasions. But the shiny brass buttons were still there, and so was the brown leather gun belt that supported a bulging, flap-covered holster and held the tunic snugly to the sergeant's waist.

"Constable Wayne is now leading a group of thirty men into the forest reserve," Sergeant Fisher told the boys as he walked with them to the side of the sandy

117

trail. "They're going to move through the bush in a straight line, walking abreast, in the hope that they'll come across Ogdeen that way. We think it very likely that he was hurt in the crash; he probably won't go too far before coming to a stop. He may be lying unconscious somewhere. By walking abreast and fairly close together, the searchers are more likely to find him if he's unconscious or dead."

The three came to a stop where car tracks left the trail and disappeared over an almost sheer drop of about sixty feet. But less than halfway down, deep skid marks began abruptly, which showed that the car had not fallen free very far, nor had it rolled. It had mainly slid, nose first, and now it hung near the bottom of the ravine amid a tangle of brush, water poplars, and willows.

Pete said, "He was lucky. Looks like the willows brought him to a cushioned stop."

"Maybe," said the sergeant, "but he must be hurt some or he would have made it back up to the road. Chances are he was somewhat stunned, and instead of climbing to the road he wandered off along the bottom of the ravine."

Don asked, "Aren't there any tracks?"

"No. The ground is very rocky down there. We're bringing in a tracking dog, but it won't be here until late tonight. I hope we find Ogdeen before that. If we don't, we may never find him. The timber wolves are bad this year. They've increased in number a lot lately, and they're roaming around all through this area. If they found an unconscious man—well, they might just overcome their natural fear of man. Excuse me for a minute. I have to make a radio call to the station." He walked toward two patrol cars parked beside the trail.

Don had heard plenty about the timber wolves which had slaughtered several calves in the community pasture that spring. The cowboys there were carrying carbines on their saddles and riding patrol at night.

Suddenly they heard the sound of an approaching vehicle, and soon Mr. Simmons's half-ton pickup rolled into sight around a bend of the pine-bordered trail.

"Took long enough," pronounced Pete.

"Julie came too," Don said.

The truck pulled to a stop. Mr. Simmons and Julie climbed out and Sergeant Fisher walked over to them. Simmons introduced him to Julie, and also explained something about being delayed because of a pig getting stuck in a fence. Don and Pete walked closer to join them.

The sergeant was saying, "I'm glad you could come. You're too late to join in the search that's going on north of here just now, but it's just as well. I can use you here, Mr. Simmons. Have you ever run a two-way radio?"

"No, sure haven't."

"There's nothing to it," smiled the Mountie. "I'll show you how to work it. You'll be keeping in touch with Constable Wayne who's leading the search—he has a portable radio with him—and you may also receive a message or two from the station. I'd like you to stay with the radio in one of our patrol cars until I return. I'm going to take these two men out to the corrals in the community pasture and organize a search on horseback from there."

"Men?" said Julie.

Everyone ignored her. The sergeant continued, "There are several cowboys with good horses at the corrals. We intend to make a thorough search of the whole pasture, all twelve square miles of it."

"I can ride," Julie said to the Mountie. "Let me help with the search in the pasture."

"There may be an extra horse at the corrals," said the Mountie, "and we need every rider we can get." He looked at Mr. Simmons.

"Fine," said Julie's father. "She's a good rider."

"Mr. Simmons, you probably know this Anthony Ogdeen as well as anyone else from around there where he lives," the sergeant said. "What's he like? I've been told he's a bit of an oddball."

"Yeah, I guess you could say that," replied Mr. Simmons. "The man is definitely mentally ill."

"What makes you say that?"

"Ask anybody around who's had anything to do with him," said Simmons. "Ask John Korely; he runs the U.G.G. elevator in town. Ask Phil Labreque who runs the store. Or ask my son here, or Don. They've all had some experience with Anthony Ogdeen. They

know how he can lose his temper for no good reason,
an' how strange he is. For instance, he paints stacks of
pictures of people gettin' slaughtered. He can't get
along with nobody, poor man. I wish him the very
best, an' that includes wishin' that he gets to a
psychiatrist in the near future. You boys better look
into that. The man needs help."

"Well, we'll have to find him first," the sergeant
said. "Come on; I'll show you how to operate the
radio. Then the rest of us will get started on our way to
the pasture."

Two more miles of riding brought Don and Pete to
the community pasture corrals. Don had been here
twice before, so the familiar corrals, sheds, stable, and
bunkhouse gave him a good feeling of orientation.
For some time before this he hadn't been sure of his
directions, even though the sun was brightly displayed against a hot summer sky. Don was used to
calculating his whereabouts according to streets and
avenues, not according to the sun.

Sergeant Fisher and Julie were already at the corrals, for they had come in one of the two police cars.
Mr. Simmons had stayed in the other one at the scene
of the accident.

The sergeant, Julie, and four long-legged cowboys
were busy stuffing themselves with delicious-
looking food from the lowered tailgate of a pickup.

"Come and join us," invited the policeman as Don
and Pete dismounted. "Looks like you got here just in
time to help Julie and me rescue at least some of this

good food from these half-starved bronco-busters."
He said all this through a smile and a big mouthful of
ham sandwich, which made him look and sound like
anything but the stolid, poker-faced sort of Mountie
that Don had encountered in storybooks. Don wondered if the books were wrong or if Sergeant Fisher
was an exception to the rule. The officer swallowed
hard and then continued speaking with a little less
strain.

"We can thank Mr. and Mrs. Deluc for this food.
She prepared it and he brought it over. They live not
far from here, and they thought we might be getting
hungry with all our searching. Sure was nice of
them."

"Sure was," agreed Pete as he moved toward a plate
of buttered muffins. "I know Mr. and Mrs. Deluc;
they're nice people. Where's Mr. Deluc now?"

"In the barn," said the sergeant, his handsome face
once more distorted, this time with chocolate cake.
"He's saddling up a horse for Julie. Good thing he
showed up; these fellas here don't know how to saddle a horse."

Don wondered if the cowboys were long-time
friends of Sergeant Fisher or if the officer made a
practice of kidding around with people he had just
met. In any case, the cowboys seemed to like it; their
facial expressions and good-natured laughter showed
that.

But one of them, at least, wasn't going to take it all
sitting down. He was probably the lankiest of the four

and had a nose to match. Deep wrinkles in his dark face accentuated an artificial frown. He said, "I'll admit I've done a few dumb things in my life, but never yet have I tried to use spurs on a V-8 motor."

As the other three cowboys threatened to gag over thunderous bursts of laughter, Don glanced down at Sergeant Fisher's heels. Sure enough, he was wearing a neat set of nickel-plated spurs, a traditional part of the uniform and a leftover from the days when the redcoats used horses instead of cars and airplanes.

Sergeant Fisher took it with an embarrassed smile. "Well, at least today my spurs will look more in place." His face grew serious as he gazed out across the vast expanse of pastureland east of the corrals. "We sure have a lot of riding to do!"

"It ain't nothin' for us," said the long-nosed cowboy, "but you'll be sloopin' on your stomach tonight."

Once mounted, the group split into separate parties. Three of the cowboys, regular riders for the pasture, were to work their way across to the other boundary, checking bushes and ravines on the way. Sergeant Fisher and the long-nosed cowboy would ride together along the fence line, one on each side of it, and in that way would comb the heavier windbreak bush that grew there. Don, Pete, and Julie would do the same thing, going around the pasture in the other direction. All three parties were to meet on the far side. Sergeant Fisher had no qualms about leaving the teenagers on their own. He had found out that Pete knew the country as well as any of the pasture riders;

also, the sergeant had learned that Don had taken an advanced course in first aid. All three mounted parties were well equipped with first-aid materials.

Pete, Don, and Julie never did meet the others on the far side of the pasture.

"Whoa!" Pete commanded his horse. Then he called out to Don and Julie who were working their way through heavy brush on the other side of the fence, the outer side. "Pull up a minute and sit quiet. I want to listen."

As Don and Julie obeyed they became aware of the sound that had caught Pete's attention. It was a raucous, screeching, unpleasant sound, but far enough in the distance to keep it from being distinct.

Pete, though, had no trouble identifying it. "Magpies," he said. "They're somewhere up ahead, probably fairly close to the fence."

Several days before Don had seen a few of the long-tailed, black and white birds on the farmyard, pecking around at the manure pile behind the barn. Their sinister postures and movements had given him the heebie-jeebies, partly because he had heard that they have been known to eat animals alive, if the animal was hurt and not able to defend itself.

The raucous pandemonium increased in volume.

"There must be an awful lot of them," said Don.

Pete's face, just for once, had entirely lost its habitual expression of cheerfulness. "They've found something," he said. "Let's move, fast!" And he dug heels into the sides of his horse.

12

The Riverbanks

Pete galloped his horse along the fence line of the Riverside Community Pasture. As soon as Don and Julie, on the other side of the fence, got their horses clear of the heavy brush, they also spurred forward at breakneck speed. Ducking poplar branches, and with their horses occasionally jumping windfalls, Don and the girl did their best to keep Pete in sight.

The screeching of the magpies grew louder so that now they could be heard even above the pounding of the horses' hoofs.

Although Don, like the other two, was doing his best to get to the flock of carnivorous birds as quickly as possible, something inside of him seemed to be turning back and running in the opposite direction. Would Ogdeen already be mutilated beyond help? There was nothing to do but hurry on and find out.

Pete pulled his horse to a skidding stop when he came in close sight of the wheeling, hovering, de-

scending, and ascending birds. About half of them
were on the ground at any one time. Altogether there
were only a couple dozen, but they were very noisy
and very busy.

Don and Julie now also arrived, breaking free of
bush and reining their horses to a stop in the little
clearing filled with clamorous avian activity. The
center of action was on their side of the fence.

The magpies were startled by the sudden appearance of three riders. Screeching even louder than they
had been, they rose like a black and white cloud
toward the two highest treetops. There they jostled
one another to find perching area. They had no intention of leaving their gruesome enterprise, expecting
this intrusion to be only a temporary interference.

The dead sheep looked more like a woolen blanket.
His wool had been plucked by the hungry birds and
spread about.

"What a relief!" said Pete. "I really expected to find
Ogdeen. What a relief!"

"You better believe it!" said Julie.

Don dismounted to check his saddle cinch. He was
afraid that the fast riding and jumping over windfalls
might have caused the saddle to shift. Seeing Don's
wise forethought, Julie did the same; then she led her
horse through a space between bushes into an adjoin-
ing clearing and was soon out of sight. Apparently
she wasn't willing to slow down in the search for
Ogdeen even for a moment. But in a few seconds she
was back and went over to Pete who still sat in his

saddle close on the other side of the fence. He and Don were discussing whether or not they should go back over the distance through which they had ridden at a gallop, in order to check that stretch more carefully.

"Look what I found," said Julie as she handed a small, dark object up to Pete.

"A book of matches," said Pete.

"Maybe Ogdeen dropped it," suggested Julie.

"Not much chance," replied Pete, handing the paper matches back to her. "Probably Mr. Deluc or his hired man dropped it. That's his land you're standing on—it borders the community pasture for several miles here—and that's his sheep."

"*Was* his sheep, you mean," corrected Julie. "Poor thing. Wonder what happened to it."

"By the looks of it, I'd say a wolf got it," offered Pete. "He ate his fill and left the rest for the magpies. Or he may have been scared off somehow before he was done with it."

Don took the matchbook from Julie's hand. When he flipped open the cover he saw something the other two hadn't noticed. Someone had been doodling with a pencil on the inside of the cover. There was a tiny sketch, very rough but quite decipherable. The miniature drawing depicted two men, one with both hands on the other's throat, clearly in the process of choking him to death. Don looked up at Pete. "This belongs to Ogdeen. You can count on it."

After Don had shown the ugly little sketch to Pete and Julie they both got pretty excited about it. Pete

tied his horse to the fence and climbed through so he
could join the other two in looking for tracks. What
they did find almost immediately was the cold re-
mains of a campfire, only a few yards from where Julie
had picked up the matchbook. It seemed likely that
Ogdeen had built the fire to warm himself sometime
during the past night.

Don, Pete, and Julie spread their search for tracks to
all sides of the ashes, but the heavy grass in the clearing had sprung back consistently so that there was no
sign of anyone having walked over it.

Julie had just suggested that they ride to tell
Sergeant Fisher about their discovery of the campfire
and matchbook when Pete found some tracks a little
ways into the surrounding poplar bush. Here there
was no grass, only a thick layer of old leaves. The shoe
prints—big enough to have been made by Ogdeen
—were very clear. Pete found something else. On a
tree trunk near the tracks was a smear of blood. It was
dry and dark-looking, but Pete said he had seen dried
blood before and that was what it looked like.

"He could be hurt pretty badly," said Pete in a
worried tone. "He probably cut his head during the
car crash and has been going around half stunned
ever since. He must have stumbled and banged his
bloody head against this tree. And it looks like he fell
down. See the way the leaves are mussed up here? But
sooner or later he must have made it back to his feet
and walked away."

Julie said, "Then the sooner we get help, the better."

"But he may be just a little ways from here," said Pete. "The important thing is for someone to get to him as soon as possible. All right, you go get Sergeant Fisher; Don and I will take the first-aid kit and follow the tracks—if we can find enough of them to lead us anywhere. And if we find Ogdeen, one of us will come back to this spot and show the sergeant where to go."

Julie climbed through the fence and took the horse that Pete had been riding—it was really hers—and started off at a gallop into the pasture. She followed a course that she hoped would bring her to Sergeant Fisher as quickly as possible.

Don and Pete found more tracks without hardly trying. Leading their horses, they followed along natural avenues between thickets of poplars and willows. Whoever had made the tracks had been taking the path of least resistance, so the going was fairly easy. The ground began to slope downward more and more.

"We're getting close to the river," said Pete.

"Do you think there's a danger of Ogdeen stumbling into the river and drowning?"

"Sure. Especially since that heavy rain. And there was another big shower here last night. Someone told my dad that the banks close to the river are a solid washout."

"What do you mean?"

"Mud," said Pete, "just a mass of mud. We'll have to be careful not to get into it ourselves."

The tracks led them out of bush and down the middle of a descending gully. There was no mud here because the soil was sandy.

"Listen," said Don. "Isn't that the sound of the river?"

"Right. Look, there's not much chance that Ogdeen climbed up the sides of this gully. I'm pretty sure he continued walking along the bottom of it. So let's get on our horses and get to the end of the gully as quick as we can. Then we'll stop and look for tracks. If we can't find any, we can always come back here to pick them up again."

"Good idea," Don said approvingly as he swung up on Pedro. The bay gelding could tell by the manner of mounting that speed was demanded, so he lowered his hindquarters in preparation to spring into a gallop. But Don suddenly held him back. "Pete! Did you hear that?"

Pete had a hard time holding back his horse. "Eh? Hear what?"

Before Don could answer, the sound he had heard came again, louder this time. Someone was shouting.

"That's Ogdeen!" said Pete. "He's calling for help! Let's go!"

They raced neck on neck along the slightly sloping gully. When they drew near the curtain of foliage that more or less closed off the end of it, Don pulled back on Pedro's reins and let Pete take the lead. It seemed like trying to commit suicide to go charging in among trees at this speed.

Pete also slowed somewhat, but not enough to break his horse's gallop. Ducking branches, he had soon passed through the narrow strip of bush. Don held his head low on Pedro's neck and followed. As he emerged onto an open hillside he was just in time to see Pete's horse slipping, losing its balance. It was a startling sight—a rearing, sliding horse and a partially unseated rider against a background of blue sky, swirling river, and black mud.

Pete left the saddle altogether and hit the mud, rolling. The horse also went down, flat on its side. Don was watching this action so intently that he hardly noticed his own horse going lower in the back. But when Pedro sat down completely and slid several yards through the mud that way, Don was forced to grab hold of the saddle horn to keep from falling backward. A few seconds later Pedro had regained all four legs and was standing quietly. Don continued to clutch the horn with a vicious grip even though there was no longer any need for it.

Pete's horse was also back on its feet now, apparently unhurt, but Pete was lying motionless in the mud.

Don jumped from the saddle and ran toward his friend. But before he got to him, the farm boy raised himself up on his elbows and looked around with a bewildered expression on his mud-plastered face.

"Pete! Are you all right?" Don knelt beside him.

After a moment, and without too much difficulty, Pete worked himself up to a sitting position. "What did you say?"

"Are you all right?"

"I'm OK. I guess that mud slapped me in the face kind of hard. But I don't even have a nosebleed, so I guess my nose isn't broken. I feel kind of stunned though."

Don was just going to ask Pete if he thought his legs were all right, but at that moment the sound of Anthony Ogdeen's voice came from somewhere not far below the muddy hillside. It was definitely Ogdeen's voice. "Help! I'm over here! This way!"

In two seconds Pete was standing up.

"I'm glad you're all right," said Don.

"Sure, I'm OK." Pete headed toward his horse with long strides, but he looked a little wobbly.

Both boys mounted and proceeded, with less speed and more caution, down the slippery hillside. Pete called out to let Ogdeen know that someone was coming to his aid. They felt fortunate in finding a gravelly outcropping that wound along the riverbank for a distance. Then, as they followed it, they noticed Ogdeen's tracks. He had walked along this same sandy ridge. It was almost like a mountain-goat trail now. On one side the muddy bank angled up sharply, and on the other side it sloped down toward the swirling current of the North Saskatchewan River.

Pete had told Don that in the language of the Cree Indians of this area, the name *Saskatchewan* means "fast-running waters." Don decided the river had been well named. But actually, though Don didn't realize it, the current was not that swift all over. Here the river was somewhat narrower and had a bend, so that the inner side of the curve, where Don and Pete were, displayed exceptionally rapid water.

The outcropping widened a bit—to about four feet—but the gravel was looser here, so the horses continued to pick their way with nervous caution around the curving hillside.

"I'm down here!" came the voice of Anthony Ogdeen. "Here I am!"

Pete and Don pulled to a sharp stop as they swung their eyes toward the river.

Ogdeen was on the bank about twenty-five feet below the gravel ridge. Obviously he had slipped over the edge and slid downward through mud. He was lying on his stomach on the steep bank, his feet toward the river, and was looking up with a sad expression on his round face. His forehead was crusted with dried blood.

"I'm afraid to move," said Ogdeen.

It was hardly a wonder that he was afraid to move, for directly behind his feet the mud slide became a vertical drop. Thirty feet straight below rushed the angry current of the North Saskatchewan.

13

Cliff-Hanger

Don and Pete quickly dismounted.

"Don't worry, Mr. Ogdeen, we'll get you back up," Pete called down to the imperiled artist. "Keep lying very still—just as you are now." He turned to his saddle and began to unbuckle a lariat. Don felt a bit useless as he stood by and watched, but he was glad to see Pete taking the situation in hand so capably. A line assist, realized Don—thinking in the lingo of his own water-safety training—was certainly what this situation called for, and the lariat made a perfect throwing line.

As Don looked down at the unfortunate Ogdeen lying there helplessly, the boy couldn't help but see the matter as a great triumph of justice. He tried to keep from being carried away with the feeling of satisfaction. Only a few days ago Ogdeen had caused him to get caught in a furious storm and the deadly, raging waters of a flood. Now the maniac was danger-

134

ously trapped by mud from that same storm. It was justice all right; he sure had this coming to him.

"Don! Come hold my horse! He's getting spooky." There was a note of harshness in Pete's voice. "We've no time to lose!"

Don quickly obeyed. "Sure, I'll make him stand still," he said as he grabbed the bridle reins and held the horse's head firmly.

"That's fine; just hold him steady like that." The harshness was gone. "I'll throw the rope down to Ogdeen." Pete had fastened one end of the lariat to the saddle horn.

A careful cast placed the thirty-five-foot rope within easy reach of Ogdeen.

"There you are," said Pete. "Mr. Ogdeen, I want you to know that we're helping you in the name of Jesus Christ."

These words probably startled Don almost as much as they did Ogdeen, but they had an amazing effect on Ogdeen. He had dared raise one hand to reach for the rope; Pete's statement brought that action to a standstill in midair. Then the hand dropped back down into the mud.

Ogdeen peered upward with a very ugly expression on his face. "In that case," rasped his hoarse voice, "I refuse to be rescued!"

Pete and Don exchanged dumbfounded glances. Then Pete dropped to one knee on the brow of the gravel ridge, as if in an effort to get closer to Ogdeen.

"You can't mean it!" said Pete. "You could slide

over the edge and fall into the river at any moment. And even if you survived the fall, you're in no shape to swim. Please hurry and grab the rope and let us pull you up!"

"I can't swim a stroke," Ogdeen informed them in a voice straining with fierce pride. "If I slide and fall, I'm a goner. But in no way will I be rescued by you after what you've just said. I'd rather die ten times than humble myself the way you want me to! And besides, I've just realized that this is a perfect opportunity for me to take care of something that's been on my mind a lot lately. Well, Don Shield, how's your Christianity coming along these days?"

Don supposed that the blow on Ogdeen's head, plus whatever other ordeals he had come through since his car crash, were causing him to behave in this extrairrational manner. But irrational or not, there was something grotesque and frightening about the way this man was willing to risk his life for the false philosophy he believed in. It reminded Don of stories he had heard in recent newscasts, where terrorists went on suicide missions, killing many innocent persons and knowing that very likely they themselves would have to die for doing this. But still they did it—so powerful is the driving force of hatred.

Ogdeen continued, now speaking to Pete. "And you too, you stupid hayseed! What's your faith going to do now? Or your so-called love? You can't let me drown if you really have love, but I won't let you rescue me unless you deny your faith in Christ!" He began to laugh in a low, soft, horrible way.

Pete, for once in his life, was stumped. He turned to Don. "What'll we do?"

At the moment Don felt like saying that if Ogdeen wanted to fall into the river, then let him; but he held himself back. "I don't know," he said.

"We've got to do something!" Pete's voice was intense with desperation. Once more he called down to the victim. "Please, Mr. Ogdeen, please grab hold of the rope!"

"Not unless you give up your Christianity!" shouted Ogdeen.

Pete remained silent for a moment, thinking, maybe praying. Again he turned to Don. "What does a person do in a case like this? Of course we can't and won't deny Christ, but we can't let the man fall into the river and drown." He moved close to Don and spoke in a low voice. "After all, he's mentally ill and doesn't really know what he's saying."

"I don't know what to do," said Don, still holding the horse's head firmly, as if everything depended on that.

Pete's look of confidence and sure-handedness quickly returned. "I'll go for Sergeant Fisher; Julie may be having trouble finding him. And I'll bring him here as quickly as I can. I guess Ogdeen will let himself be rescued by Sergeant Fisher."

"I guess so," said Don.

"In the meantime do everything you can to keep

Ogdeen from getting excited. Don't mention Christianity in any form."

"No, I guess I'd better not," agreed Don.

Pete went over to Pedro and turned the quarter horse about on the narrow outcropping before mounting. In spite of the danger of loose gravel and mud, he rode off at a canter.

Don remained standing beside the other horse. When he looked down at Ogdeen he saw that the fat man was also looking at him, and now there was an expression of still greater hatred on the artist's face. Don had seen that look once before—during the night of the storm when he had told Ogdeen about the necessity of surrendering to Christ.

Now the angry man's fat lips issued a cutting flame of vulgar abuse. It was all directed at Don, and the youth felt it deeply. No one had ever before cussed him out quite that thoroughly.

"So you thought the tables had been turned on me very neatly, didn't you?" raved Ogdeen, slowing down enough to switch from straight cursing to more orthodox sentence structure. "I know exactly what you were thinking. You hate my guts for the way I've put you in your place a couple of times. Now you were thinking, 'Isn't this nice! Here's Anthony Ogdeen all covered with mud and humbled. Now all we have to do is rescue him and show him how wonderful we are, and how wonderful our religion is.' You hypocrite! No, you're not even a hypocrite; you're a fool. You think you're trying to rescue me out of kindness, but really you're doing it to get even with me. If you knew anything about how the mind works, you'd know that what I'm saying is true. But all you know about is your religion. Why am I wasting my time talking to such a fool? Well, anyhow, now you can see that your great idea of coming to the rescue of a poor, defeated unbeliever isn't working."

Don knew deep inside that he should be taking this calmly, but he felt his anger mounting with every word the artist spoke. The boy's face must have shown it, for Ogdeen began to laugh sardonically.

"A Christian, eh?" said the fat man. "Right now you'd like to kick me down into the river—if you could reach me—wouldn't you?" He laughed again.

Don didn't feel like kicking Ogdeen into the river, but he did feel like turning his back and walking away. *And maybe,* thought Don, *maybe that's almost as bad. Dear Lord,* he prayed silently, *please help me with this! Please help me to get over these bad feelings.*

Don looked out across the wide river, trying to let God's love and tranquillity sink into him. But instead of gaining peace, he felt a deeper guilt. He suddenly realized clearly that although he didn't hate Ogdeen, he also had not—especially since the night of the flood—felt anything like sincere compassion for him. God's love was reaching out to Ogdeen, Don knew, but Don's own soul had been a blocked channel. *I'm sorry,* he prayed simply.

When he looked back down at Ogdeen a few sec-

onds later, Don still didn't feel completely relieved of
anger, but he did have a strong grip on it. And now he
felt a sudden surge of true sympathy, much like what
he had experienced while witnessing to Julie. It was a
sincere, fervent feeling of reaching out toward this
mixed-up artist from Los Angeles who considered
everyone to be a fool. *Lord, how can I really help him?*

To Don's mind came the memory of words he had
once heard an evangelist use in a sermon: "God
comes to everyone on their own level." Don believed
this. It had certainly been true in his own case. He had
found peace with God through the helpful words of a
swimming instructor who was a Christian, and the
swimming pool had been on Don's level. He had more
or less lived there. Suddenly Don knew what to say to
Ogdeen.

"I guess you figure my Christian beliefs are only on
the surface. You think my subconscious mind is forcing me along this way of thinking and believing in
order to get me to the goals I've set for myself—in
other words, to fulfill the life-style that I've unconsciously chosen."

Ogdeen remained silent for several seconds, but
outside of that he covered his surprise fairly well.
Then he said, "What would you know about anything
like that? Obviously you know something, though.
That sounded a lot like Adlerian psychology you
were spouting off."

For the first time since he had begun his reading of
books on psychology and psychiatry—which he had

hoped would help him to deal more effectively with his swimming class at the mental institution—Don understood why he had felt so strongly that this study was important. He knew that God had been preparing him for this very moment. "Alfred Adler talked a lot about life-styles," said Don, "but other schools of psychology have expressed the same idea in other words."

"You don't say!" returned Ogdeen. "Now what's a Christian doing with all this worldly stuff in his head? I suppose you've studied Freud too. What do you think of him?"

"He had some pretty good ideas," said Don, "but he got kind of hung up on sex. That's just my personal opinion, of course."

"Of course. Young fellow, I must warn you; you're in great danger of becoming a heretic. You seem to have been doing some thinking, and for a Christian, that's poison." Ogdeen no longer looked angry, but his face carried an expression of hateful derision. "You could end up being burned at the stake. A Christian should never use his mind."

"Whatever gave you that idea?" returned Don. "Christianity deals with life, and thinking is a part of life, although not the most important part. Believing in God is more important."

"Ha!" said Ogdeen with such fervor that he threatened to shake himself loose from his precarious moorings. "When you start talking about blind faith, that's where you lose me."

"I'm not talking about *blind* faith," responded Don quickly, surprised at his own eagerness to carry on with this spiritual-mental duel. "There's nothing blind about believing the God who made you. He's the King of the universe and can think circles around anyone."

Ogdeen didn't answer for a moment, and as he continued to look up, a slow smile—one with a degree of sincere goodwill in it—began to shape over his face. He said, "I'm beginning to think that my first opinion of you was right after all. I think I could have some real interesting arguments with you."

14

The Mighty Saskatchewan

Pete, Julie, Sergeant Fisher, and the long-nosed cowboy rode four abreast at a hard gallop over rolling grassland in the community pasture. Although Pete's horse was only a neck in advance of the others, the farm boy was leading the party. He steered a beeline toward the riverbanks. Pete had found the group already being led by Julie, but now that he was in charge of guiding the riders they made faster progress. He knew every square inch of the pasture and could quickly find the shortest route around gullies and groves of poplar trees. Nevertheless, he did get slowed down by one long strip of bush near the edge of the grazing land. The group was forced to ride at a walk through this.

Pete and Julie became separated a little from the other two. Julie said in a voice low enough so only Pete could hear, "I'm worried about leaving Ogdeen alone with Don."

Pete looked at her sharply. "What do you mean?"

"Well, you know that Ogdeen has been pretty rough on Don. Don's probably real happy to see the guy in trouble now; and without hardly realizing what he's doing, he may purposely get Ogdeen excited and cause him to slip over the edge into the river. You said he was just barely hanging there."

"Julie, you're crazy! I'm sorry; I shouldn't have said that. But you're all wrong about Don. He's doing his best to help rescue Ogdeen."

"If you think I'm crazy, why do you have to apologize for saying so? It seems to me that Christians never say what they really mean! And Don pretends to want to rescue Ogdeen, but he doesn't really want to, because he hates him. To me this proves something. It proves there are a lot of phony Christians around. Maybe they're all phony!"

Pete was so deeply hurt by what his sister was saying that he didn't know how to answer her. After a moment of heavy silence, Julie said, "Pete, I wish I hadn't popped off at you like that. I can't help feeling mixed up about Christianity, but I'm sorry I got mad at you."

Pete could see she was being sincere and his heart went out to her. "It's all right, Julie," he said.

Moments later they came clear of the bush. Pete called back to Sergeant Fisher, "We don't have far to go from here, but let's give it all we've got. I guess we'll have to pull down the fence wires when we get to the edge of the pasture so we can get across."

Then they were once more leaning over the necks of their hard-galloping horses.

* * *

On a muddy bank above the North Saskatchewan River, Don and Anthony Ogdeen were still carrying on their strange conversation. What made it strange, mainly, was that Don was squatting on a gravel out-cropping, looking down at Ogdeen, and the artist was lying on his stomach in mud, looking up at Don. The two were separated by about twenty five feet of slick hillside. Directly behind Ogdeen's mud-caked shoes was a thirty-foot sheer drop into the swirling current of the river. The fat man was being very careful not to dislodge himself.

But he did talk. Right now he was relating how he had come to have the godless philosophy by which he lived. "I used to go to church quite a bit," he said, making it sound like a guilty confession, "but I never found it satisfying. Sometimes I'd pray— I'd ask God for things; but I didn't get the things I asked for. So I thought, what's the use of praying?"

"God doesn't always give us what we ask for," put in Don. "It'd be too bad for us if he did."

Ogdeen ignored this. "I don't mind admitting that at the time I was in bad shape emotionally and finally ended up in a mental hospital. But I got some good help there. Those psychiatrists were all right; they were intelligent persons and knew their way around emotional problems. People are afraid of psychia-trists and mental hospitals, but it so happens that mental hospitals are among the few places in the world where there's some intelligent, sensible work going on and where the doctors are willing to listen to what a person has to say. I wouldn't be afraid to go back there. If I ever thought I needed that kind of help again, I wouldn't hesitate to go back.

"Anyhow, after I got out of there I made contact with a group of freethinkers who followed the kind of philosophy that made sense to me. They helped me a lot. We had a meeting place in an apartment on Wilshire. That's the classiest business street in L.A. We got rid of the make-believe and went only according to hard facts. We're strictly materialistic—don't accept any kind of mysticism. We don't believe in God and we don't believe in love either. There's really no such thing as love—it's an illusion. Everyone is completely selfish; the only difference is that some people admit it and others don't."

"You're wrong," said Don. "Love is the greatest thing there is. If it's not real, then how come some people make sacrifices for others? Some people have even given their lives for the sake of others. And we can tell that we all need love. We all need to love and to be loved. It's kind of basic."

"It's kind of a lot of nonsense," returned Ogdeen. Then a new variety of frown settled on his face. His bruised forehead creased into sharp wrinkles. "Ooooh," he moaned. "The pain is coming back." A second later his raised head and shoulders fell forward into the mud. The movement started him slid-

ing. But only a few inches. Somehow there was
enough friction to once more bring him to a stop, now
with his feet protruding over the cliff. There he lay
motionless except for a visible heavy breathing. Obviously he was unconscious.

Don slowly let out his breath. *That was awfully
close*, he thought. Then he heard the sound of approaching hoofbeats.

When the four riders got there, Sergeant Fisher lost
no time in going ahead with the rescue. Now he
suddenly looked the way Don thought a Mountie
should look. There was no longer any unnecessary
talk or superfluous action. But there were terse orders. The cowboy was instructed to go bring a patrol
car as close to the riverbanks as possible and to carry
in a stretcher from there. To Don, the sergeant said,
"Hold the horse. Don't let him move." He was refer-
ring to the horse that still had the uncoiled lasso rope
fastened to its saddle.

Rather than take a loop around his waist, the Mountie tied the lasso to his sturdy leather gun belt, because this way he would have more rope left over to
tie around Ogdeen. With lithe, easy movements,
Sergeant Fisher lowered himself along the lariat,
bracing his boots into the mud. He had only three feet
to go when it happened.

The saddle, its girth loosened earlier by rough riding, slipped to the side because of the rope's pull. The
girth did not come undone, but with the saddle hang-

ing on the side of the horse, the lasso's loop easily slipped off the horn.

Sergeant Fisher fell back heavily against Ogdeen and sent the unconscious man sliding and rolling over the cliff's edge. As Ogdeen dropped out of sight, the Mountie was also partly over the edge and falling free. But then, with his chest still above the muddy brink, the policeman came to a jolting stop as the rope suddenly stiffened in his hands. The small loop with its metal honda—the end that had been fastened to the saddle horn—had stuck between a deeply imbedded rock and a tree stump.

But it was apparent that Sergeant Fisher wanted to free himself from the rope so that he also would drop down into the river. His intention was to rescue Ogdeen. However, the knot around the officer's gun belt was so tight that his straining fingers couldn't get it undone; and because it was positioned directly over the buckle, he couldn't unfasten the belt either.

Don knew what he had to do. He could have told himself that it was useless and foolhardy to try to catch up to the unconscious artist in that rapid current, but his overwhelming desire to help Ogdeen turned the decision into much less of a test than it might have been.

In a few seconds Don had discarded his boots, jacket, and hat and was sprinting forward off the gravel ridge. He had practiced simulated rescues so often that this didn't seem very unusual, even though he was sliding in ankle-deep mud down a riverbank instead of running along the clean cement that bordered his favorite Minneapolis swimming pool. As he bounded downward toward the brink he was automatically deciding what sort of takeoff to do. His training dictated that he jump feet first. So when he got to the edge where Sergeant Fisher was still struggling to free himself, Don leaped out into space as far as his legs could drive him.

He managed to maintain his vertical posture as he fell. Except for a quick glance he didn't look to see what awaited him below. Instead, his searching eyes were turned downstream where they were rewarded by the sight of a head, shoulders, and flailing arms. *So the shock of cold water has revived Ogdeen*, thought Don as his body rammed deep into the river.

He felt the strong current grip him. Without fighting it, he stroked diagonally to the surface, then shifted into a modified crawl with his face above water. He made for the area where he had glimpsed Ogdeen. But the artist was not in sight now. Wait! There he was, breaking surface and once more clawing frantically at thin air.

Don couldn't do his top speed for two reasons. First, he had to hold his head out of the water in an attempt to keep the victim in sight, and second, he couldn't use up all his strength now if he hoped to have any left when, and if, he got a hold of Ogdeen. Yet there wasn't much point in pulling a dead man out of the river. *I'll have to cut this pretty fine*, Don told himself. *Every second counts.*

Then, without warning, a strong undercurrent fastened icy claws on the young swimmer and dragged him downward relentlessly into the cold pressure of the Saskatchewan's depths.

Julie saw him go down. From where she and her brother sat in the mud, about four feet down from the gravel ridge, they had a clear view of the river. But Pete wasn't looking in that direction. He was busy hanging onto the lasso loop to make sure it didn't slip out from between the rock and the stump. Pete braced his feet against the rock and pulled up on the loop a few inches so that he himself held the weight of the police officer. Sergeant Fisher now had his feet back on the muddy bank and was carefully climbing up.

"Don't worry, Sergeant," Pete said through clenched teeth. "Keep climbing. This rope is going to stay right here."

Julie said, "He went under, and he hasn't come back up." There was a quavering note of desperation in her voice.

Pete thought she was talking about Ogdeen. "Leave him to Don," he said. "That's all we can do now."

"No," said Julie, "I *mean* Don—I saw him go down and he hasn't come back up! The current is too strong for him." Her voice broke into a sob.

"Never mind that now," said Pete brusquely. "Just keep anchoring me down. If this rope slips there'll be one or two more people in the river."

Julie hung her slight weight more effectively on Pete's wide shoulders, but her mind could not be pried away from its bent. "I was all wrong about Don," she murmured. "And now I'll probably never see him again—alive. And I was all wrong when I said Christians are mostly hypocrites. I know now that I was only looking for an excuse to keep from becoming a Christian myself. But I'm sorry. Pete, do you hear me? I'm sorry."

Pete's voice was gentle. "Better tell God about that."

Sergeant Fisher pulled himself upward along the rope one more arm length and then got a grip on the stump.

The current sucked Don downward, tumbling him along like a dead fish. As the depth increased, so did the cold and the darkness. But abruptly he felt himself pressed painlessly against something—he didn't know what. It was strange. After that he seemed to have become much stabilized, even though the water was still rushing violently all about him. He calculated that he was in a head-down position but wasn't sure. One thing was sure; if he intended to stay alive he had to get to air—fast!

Don struggled hard and was almost surprised to find the water turning paler around him. He was nearing the surface. Fortunately the down current had grown weaker, but something other than water was pulling at him, tangling around his arms and legs.

His head broke clear into bright sunlight and sweet air. It took a few moments of deep, delicious breath-

ing before he returned to his normal senses enough to
realize that he was tangled in fishnet. He knew the net
must be anchored or snagged somewhere, for it had
brought his underwater journey to a stop.

Ogdeen was also tangled in the net, not more than
five yards away from Don.

The fat artist was still conscious and still struggling. Don knew that Ogdeen's surplus weight,
which rendered him more buoyant than the average
person, had contributed a lot to his survival up to this
point. But it was also plain that he couldn't last much
longer. He was flopping around like a harpooned
whale, and his head was under water about as much
as above.

Don got himself clear of the fishnet without too
much difficulty or loss of time. When he tried freeing
the drowning man, however, it was a different matter.
The net itself wouldn't have been so bad, but as Don
moved in closer, the frantic Ogdeen suddenly
reached out and wrapped his big arms around Don's
neck in a crushing headlock.

Don tucked in his chin as much as he could and
submerged, taking Ogdeen along, That should have
been enough to undo the hold, but just then the
drowning man's arms went into a convulsive, tight-
ening spasm, probably indicating the approach of
unconsciousness. With the grip still tighter now,
Don's pulse-pounding head took on a giddy feeling.
In desperation he began a more concentrated release
method, knowing that if it failed there was nothing

more he could do to free himself from the steellike arms that encircled his head and neck and wrestled him down into the river.

He placed his hands on Ogdeen's midsection and pushed the large, net-entangled form up and away from him. This automatically forced Don still deeper below the surface of the water, and with Ogdeen horizontal now, his stranglehold became much less secure.

Don did a quick, violent shrug with his shoulders and broke the hold completely.

In a second he was directly below Ogdeen. A simultaneous push and pull by the boy's hands turned the drowning man face up. Stroking hard, Don now swam up beside Ogdeen and drew him to the surface.

Don quickly put him into a cross-chest-carry position. One arm was clamped across Ogdeen's chest, and the youth's upper hip was in the small of the other's back supporting him firmly. The fishnet still clung to the big man, but as Don poured all the strength he had left into a scissors kick and a shallow arm pull, he and his burden broke free.

By now the young swimmer was so tired that he almost missed seeing a sandbar—one of the reefs common to this river—about twenty yards to his right. It was a long, narrow island of gravel, sand, and silt that the coursing water had piled up over a period of months or years. Without fighting the current too much, Don angled in toward the bar. He came close to missing it, but got the tail end. Heart pounding and lungs wheezing, he dragged Ogdeen up on dry ground.

The artist had stopped breathing. Although Don knew that every second counted heavily, he had no choice but to catch his own breath before he could apply mouth-to-mouth artificial respiration. But when he did proceed, Ogdeen quickly responded. He regained his breathing and most of his consciousness simultaneously. Don quickly turned him onto his side, propping a knee against his back to steady him; and he supported the man's head in a face-downward position. For a while Don began to think Ogdeen had swallowed half the North Saskatchewan River. Finally he ran dry. After that his breathing became regular and natural.

With Ogdeen still on his side, Don continued to squat beside him so he could keep a careful eye on the man's breathing. And it was during this time that the youth decided he would do all in his power to see that Ogdeen was committed to a mental hospital where he'd be able to receive the treatment he needed so much. Ogdeen was still a citizen of the United States, so maybe he could be committed to the institution in Minneapolis where Don had worked as a volunteer. That seemed like a really good idea, for some of the psychiatrists there were followers of Christ who always did their best to help the patients spiritually as well as mentally.

Don expected to be working there again in the fall, so possibly he'd have many opportunities to talk to

Ogdeen if they could somehow get him there. One optimistic note was the way Ogdeen had expressed positive feelings about mental hospitals, saying that he'd be willing to go back to one anytime he thought he needed that kind of help. Well, someone would have to convince him that he needed help now.

Don had been watching over the semiconscious man for some minutes when a loud shout sounded across the strip of swirling water that separated the sandbar from the riverbank. It was Sergeant Fisher. He was there close to the water's edge, and so was Julie.

The Mountie called, "Don! Don, we'll get to you as soon as we can. Pete has gone to look for a canoe or boat. Is Ogdeen alive?"

Don yelled back that Ogdeen was OK, but that he needed warmth and a place of greater comfort to help fight off the danger of shock.

"We'll do all we can!" called Sergeant Fisher.

Now Julie's pretty voice floated out over the river, and the water's telephonic ability made her words seem very near. "Don, I'm so glad you're all right. When you get off that sandbar, I have something to tell you."

Don waved to her in acknowledgment. She seemed very happy and it made him wonder.

"I would assume," spoke up the husky voice of Anthony Ogdeen, "that as a swimmer you've already graduated from the paddling pool class." He made a motion to turn onto his back, so Don let him.

"That's true," Don replied smoothly, "but I did start out in a paddling pool."

After that Ogdeen remained silent for a while, lying very still and looking up at Don. The artist's face was expressionless. Then he asked, "Did you rescue me in the name of Jesus Christ?"

"Yes," said Don, "and with the help of God."

There was another long pause before Anthony Ogdeen said, "Sometime we'll have to have another good argument about things like that—if it's all right with you."

"Anytime," said Don.